LAST CHANCE

Fargo knew they had reached the crisis point, and at first all seemed lost. Fargo had depleted his spare cylinder, too, and despite having killed or wounded more than half the attackers, he and Booger had no time to reload. A movement in the corner of his eye made Fargo glance toward the rear of the coach just in the nick of time to spot Red Sash with his knife cocked back to throw—in the desperate confusion, he had managed to ride around on the south flank and leap onto the coach.

Fargo rolled hard and fast as Red Sash threw his knife, grabbing the express gun and cocking both hammers. Sprawled on his back, Fargo fired both barrels almost point-blank. The twin load of buckshot lifted the Apache off the coach in a bloody spray. . . .

THE TRAILSMAN
#376

NEW MEXICO MADMAN

by

Jon Sharpe

A SIGNET BOOK

SIGNET
Published by New American Library, a division of
Penguin Group (USA) Inc., 375 Hudson Street,
New York, New York 10014, USA
Penguin Group (Canada), 90 Eglinton Avenue East, Suite 700, Toronto,
Ontario M4P 2Y3, Canada (a division of Pearson Penguin Canada Inc.)
Penguin Books Ltd., 80 Strand, London WC2R 0RL, England
Penguin Ireland, 25 St. Stephen's Green, Dublin 2,
Ireland (a division of Penguin Books Ltd.)
Penguin Group (Australia), 250 Camberwell Road, Camberwell, Victoria 3124,
Australia (a division of Pearson Australia Group Pty. Ltd.)
Penguin Books India Pvt. Ltd., 11 Community Centre, Panchsheel Park,
New Delhi - 110 017, India
Penguin Group (NZ), 67 Apollo Drive, Rosedale, Auckland 0632,
New Zealand (a division of Pearson New Zealand Ltd.)
Penguin Books (South Africa) (Pty.) Ltd., 24 Sturdee Avenue,
Rosebank, Johannesburg 2196, South Africa

Penguin Books Ltd., Registered Offices:
80 Strand, London WC2R 0RL, England

First published by Signet, an imprint of New American Library,
a division of Penguin Group (USA) Inc.

First Printing, February 2013
10 9 8 7 6 5 4 3 2 1

The first chapter of this book previously appeared in *Texas Swamp Fever*, the three
hundred seventy-fifth volume in this series.

Copyright © Penguin Group (USA) Inc., 2013

 REGISTERED TRADEMARK—MARCA REGISTRADA

Printed in the United States of America

PUBLISHER'S NOTE
This is a work of fiction. Names, characters, places, and incidents either are the
product of the author's imagination or are used fictitiously, and any resemblance to
actual persons, living or dead, business establishments, events, or locales is entirely
coincidental.
    The publisher does not have any control over and does not assume any respon-
sibility for author or third-party Web sites or their content.

ALWAYS LEARNING   **PEARSON**

The Trailsman

Beginnings . . . they bend the tree and they mark the man. Skye Fargo was born when he was eighteen. Terror was his midwife, vengeance his first cry. Killing spawned Skye Fargo, ruthless, cold-blooded murder. Out of the acrid smoke of gunpowder still hanging in the air, he rose, cried out a promise never forgotten.

The Trailsman they began to call him all across the West: searcher, scout, hunter, the man who could see where others only looked, his skills for hire but not his soul, the man who lived each day to the fullest, yet trailed each tomorrow. Skye Fargo, the Trailsman, the seeker who could take the wildness of a land and the wanting of a woman and make them his own.

*New Mexico Territory, 1860—where Fargo serves
as bodyguard for "America's Sweetheart"
on a stagecoach bound straight for hell.*

1

"When I was still just a lad wearing short pants, Olney, I found a sparrow with a broken wing. I picked it up and held it trapped in one hand. Have you ever held a small bird captive in your fist?"

While he spoke, Zack Lomax stood in the embrasure of a bay window looking out upon Santa Fe's fashionable College Street. When no answer was forthcoming, he spun around suddenly to stare at his subordinate.

"Well? *Have* you, man?"

Olney Lucas glanced quickly away from those intense, burning-coal eyes. "No, boss, I never done that."

"Well, you should try it sometime because it's an immense thrill of power. Even as a kid I felt it—like I was God in the universe, see? I could feel its tiny heart racing like the mechanism of a fine Swiss watch. And suddenly I realized I was the master of life and death. One good squeeze and I could cancel that sparrow's existence forever. The thrill it gave me . . . later, as a man, not even the glory of the rut can match that thrill."

Lomax laced his fingers behind his back and began pacing the fancy Persian carpet in his study. He was of middle height, built solid as a meetinghouse, and well turned out in a dark wool suit with satin facings on the lapels. His hard, angular, shrewdly intelligent face featured fiercely burning eyes of limitless ambition and brooding obsession. Eyes few men could meet for more than a second or two without being unnerved and looking away.

"I'm a man now, Olney, not a lad in short pants. And the new sparrow in my hand is a vicious, supercilious bitch named Kathleen Barton. 'America's Sweetheart.' In a pig's

1

ass! Do you have *any* idea what that self-loving, stuck-up thespian bitch cost me?"

Olney had worked for Lomax long enough to know which questions required answers. Lomax would answer this one himself, just as he had hundreds of times since that fateful day, almost one year ago, in San Francisco.

"That goddamn election was *mine*!" Lomax fumed. "Bought and paid for. I had the Barbary Coast Hounds on my payroll and half the aldermen blackmailed. Think of it, Olney—Mayor of San Francisco! California itself was the next prize, and with slavery legalized there I would have run an empire. That ball-breaking twat cost me all of it. *All* of it! Turned me into a national laughingstock afraid to show my face in public."

For Lomax, who had never brooked a slight in his life, this was no old wound, but a fresh scab being torn off every day. He felt rage and shame searing into him anew. Plenty of men had proposed marriage to beautiful women and been given the mitten. But he had made the fatally overconfident mistake of proposing to Kathleen Barton on the front page of *The Californian*—a grandiose gesture he was sure would sweep the alluring actress off her feet.

Instead, she had ruined him every way but financially. Her scathing letter of rejection—also front-page newspaper fare—had described him as "a criminal beast who deserves public flogging" and assured her adoring public she "would rather kiss a toad than let that despicable, corrupt scoundrel ever touch me."

With one devastating letter his hopes for controlling the Bear Flag Republic were reduced to mere mental vapors. And thanks to this new Associated Press for the sharing of telegraphic dispatches, his shame and ruin had become a national—eventually even international—cause célèbre. Too humiliated to even face the society he once dominated, he'd pulled his hat from the political ring to avoid a landslide defeat.

"Well, the fancy bitch had her fun," Lomax declared now, still furiously pacing. "But you know my anthem, Olney: Whoever does not submit to the rudder must submit to the rock."

"Sure, boss. But is it such a good idea to kill her on the first anniversary of her letter? I mean, Christ! It's a fingerboard pointing right at you."

"Sell your ass. All the world knows that Zack Lomax was supposedly killed in an explosion at one of his own San Francisco breweries. Here in Santa Fe I'm Cort Bergman, mining investor. No one will even make the connection. And everyone knows that beautiful, popular theater actresses are magnets for unstable admirers. Her death will never be traced to me—except that *she* will know. I'll make damn sure of that."

Shaking off his familiar, acid-bitter rage, Lomax suddenly became all business. "You've followed my instructions to the letter?"

Olney nodded. "Russ Alcott swears by all things holy that we can trust this informer. He's high up in Overland's New Mexico Division. Kathleen Barton used a fake name and wore a veil, but she's too famous and he recognized her. She's booked passage for the El Paso to Santa Fe run day after tomorrow."

A hard-lipped smile straight as a seam divided Lomax's face. "That rings right. Her performance at El Paso's Palacio Theater has just closed, and she's opening here in town at the Bella Union in just twelve days. Have you set up the mirror-relay system?"

"All set. Just like the army uses out here. As long as the sun's shining, you and Alcott can communicate quick as a finger snap."

Lomax looked pleased. "Any new word on special security arrangements for her?"

Olney Lucas fortified himself with a deep breath. *Stand by for the blast*, he warned himself.

"Well, you were right, boss. There'll be no military escort. Overland's Division Manager, and the bitch's agent, don't want no attention drawn to the run. Soldiers usually escort bullion runs, and they don't want to lure Mexican freebooters."

He hesitated, and Lomax alerted like a hound on point. "What is it?" he demanded sharply.

"Well, the thing of it is—according to Alcott's report,

3

this theater agent won't be traveling with her. He's hired on Skye Fargo as the shotgun rider. Actually, as Barton's bodyguard."

For a moment Lomax looked as if he'd been slugged hard but not quite dropped. He stopped pacing, and for a full thirty seconds stood as still as a pillar of salt, his face going pale as fresh linen.

"Fargo!" He spat the word out like a bad taste. "The 'savage angel' as the fawning newspaper scribblers call him. The 'man whom bees will not sting.' "

"Maybe bees *can* sting him, but it's a hard-cash fact that he's left a trail of graves all over the West. He's hell on two sticks."

Lomax seemed to gather himself, squaring his shoulders and regaining some color in his face. "No question about it, Olney, he's no man to take lightly. In fact, if we are not meticulously careful, Skye Fargo is the rock we'll split on. But I planned for something like this. For *one full year* I've worked this out."

Lomax resumed pacing like a caged tiger. "Fargo is famous for his prowess as a killer, certainly. But often he wins the day by a simple strategy: always mystify, mislead and surprise your enemies. By a happy coincidence, that's *our* strategy, too."

Olney perked up at this reminder. "By God, it is, ain't it?"

"We're attacking our opponent at his greatest strength. And don't forget, neither Fargo nor anyone else knows we have an informer inside Overland. And wouldn't you agree that Russ, Cleo and Spider are first-rate killers?"

"Just like Fargo—no men to fool with, boss. In Lincoln County they call Russ Alcott the Widow Maker. I've seen him light matches with a pistol at twenty feet. And he handpicked those two siding him."

Lomax nodded. "Fargo can't possibly know we'll have a paid killer on that coach, too, as our ace in the hole. Or even that we know exactly *which* run Kathleen will be on. If they switch runs at the last minute, we'll know that also."

"The way you say, boss. But no matter how you slice it, there's no killing the woman until we put the quietus on

4

Fargo. And slick plan or no, when it comes to *that* job, it'd be easier to put socks on a rooster."

Again Lomax nodded. "Never underrate your enemy. The road to hell is paved with the bones of fools who made that mistake. I won't. *One year*, Olney. Night and day, planning even for something as formidable as Skye Fargo. But the suspense clock has been set ticking: exactly eleven days from now, on June nineteenth, 1860, Kathleen Suzanne Barton will draw her ultimate breath in this world."

He crossed to a huge mahogany desk and picked up a Spanish dagger featuring a jewel-encrusted, hammered-silver hilt.

"Fargo first, of course, and I don't give a damn who kills him or how. And then, ten miles west of this City of Holy Faith . . . at a spot appropriately named Blood Mesa. First, I'll watch the terror ignite in her eyes—make that proud, haughty beauty beg and grovel, perhaps even piss herself. Next, I'll shred that breathtakingly beautiful face, and then I'll carve her goddamn stone heart out of her chest. Just the way she cut mine out back in San Francisco."

By now Lomax was breathing so hard his breath whistled faintly in his nostrils.

"Boss?" Olney said quietly.

It took Lomax a long moment to realize his lackey had spoken. "Yes?"

"Just curious. That bird you caught when you was a kid— what happened to it?"

Lomax's lips twitched. He held one open hand out, then suddenly squeezed it into a tight fist. "Master of life and death, Olney. Just like God in the universe."

2

"Mr. Fargo, this job will *not* be coffee-cooler's furlough," warned Addison Steele, Manager of the New Mexico Division of Overland Stage and Freighting. "If Mr. Jenkins here is correct in his surmise, you will most definitely be earning your ten dollars a day."

Ten dollars a day, Fargo repeated to himself. Nobody paid that kind of money for anything short of a suicide mission. But at the moment, the fiddle-footed frontiersman didn't have two half dimes to rub together. And even a man who preferred the emptiest corner of the canyon needed money now and then.

Fargo, Steele and a theatrical manager from back east named Ambrose Jenkins occupied a small back office of Overland's El Paso depot. Jenkins cultivated a neat, waxed mustache and wore his hair parted in the middle, shiny with macassar oil. He had a brisk, take-charge manner that irritated Fargo.

"Addison is not being melodramatic, Fargo," Jenkins said. "Kathleen Barton's life is not only in danger—I suspect the man who intends to kill her is none other than Zack Lomax."

Fargo, comfortably seated in a leather-upholstered wing chair, crossed his ankles and narrowed his eyes as he tried to recollect the name. His face was tanned hickory-nut brown above the darker brown of his close-cropped beard.

"Lomax . . . Lomax. Say, wasn't he the jasper who died awhile back in an explosion out in San Francisco?"

"That's the story his people put out, yes. But the body they supplied was burned beyond any recognition. Neither I nor my client, Miss Barton, ever quite believed it."

"I read something about him," Fargo said. "Owned half of San Francisco and crooked as cat shit."

"He's been painted as the blackest man in that corrupt city," Addison Steele put in, "and that hellhole has no dearth of scoundrels, as you well know."

Enlightenment suddenly touched Fargo's face and he straightened his long, buckskin-clad legs, leaning forward in the chair.

"*Hell* yes, I remember it now—it was a helluva stirring-and-to-do. Lomax got him a powerful yen for this actress and the damn knot head popped the question in a newspaper instead of privately. She turned him down in a letter to the same crap sheet, and Lomax looked like a bigger fool than God made him."

"Turned him down?" Jenkins repeated, his tone mocking the phrase. "Fargo, she turned that rooster into a capon. He was not only forced to quit the mayoral race—which he practically had in the bag—but he became the butt of the biggest joke in the city."

"All right," Fargo said. "But what proof you got that he's alive and means to kill your client?"

"As to actual proof, nothing the law deems probative. But this explosion happened only weeks after her letter, and as I said, the body could have been anyone. More to the point, the anonymous letter she recently received quoted the Old Testament: 'Behold, the day cometh.' And later this month—the nineteenth, to be exact—marks the first anniversary of her now famous letter."

"Interesting," was all Fargo said.

"Jenkins believes the scoundrel is somewhere in this area," Steele added, "probably flourishing under a summer name. He almost certainly has deep reserves of capital. And he's a highly resourceful man known for intricate planning."

"Resourceful enough," Fargo put in, "to know exactly *which* stagecoach she'll be taking?"

"That seems unlikely," Steele replied. "Her fellow passengers will certainly recognize her eventually. But she purchased her tickets in disguise under the name Roberta Davis. I wish she had let someone else purchase them for her, but she's a very . . . self-sufficient woman."

Fargo looked puzzled. "Tickets? You mean for her and Jenkins?"

"I'm not going," Jenkins replied, looking injured.

"As I'm sure you know, Mr. Fargo," Steele explained, "our western Concords are large, sturdy, Wells Fargo–style models that seat nine passengers in three seats. The front and middle seats face each other. Evidently, Miss Barton always purchases three tickets so she'll have the rear seat all to herself."

"Seems a mite queer," Fargo opined, "given the sky-high price of a stagecoach ticket."

Jenkins cleared his throat. "You must understand, Fargo, that Kathleen Barton is a superlative artist—unsurpassed in all of American theater and worshipped abroad. But the warm, vivacious persona she projects on stage is just that—a persona. The woman herself is . . . well, to put it bluntly, elitist and disdainful of the common man."

"Common men like me, you mean?"

Jenkins surveyed Fargo, taking in the sweat-stained red bandanna around his throat, the bullet-holed white hat on his knee, the wicked Arkansas toothpick projecting from a boot sheath. And those dark stains in some of the fringes of his buckskins—animal blood or human?

"Well, I'd hardly call you a 'common' man or I wouldn't have hired you," Jenkins said diplomatically. "But this brings up another delicate matter. One concerning your . . . ahh, amorous proclivities."

"My . . . ahh who?"

Addison Steele hid a grin behind his hand. "Ambrose means your famous reputation, Fargo, as a mattress acrobat."

Jenkins frowned at this crude bluntness but nodded agreement.

"Fargo, you must understand," he explained. "More than most beautiful women of her profession, Kathleen Barton takes great pleasure in putting the crusher on men—as she did Lomax. Even fabulously wealthy European noblemen have wooed her only to be humiliated. A man of your station, completely lacking in social background, education and financial success, must at all times avoid any attempt at intimacy. You are her 'bodyguard' in only one connotation of the word—to protect her from harm."

Fargo was a mere jobber, interested only in the money, and didn't care a frog's fat ass whether or not some high-toned stage princess snooted him. But Jenkins grated on his nerves so he decided to rowel him a little.

"Oh, I don't know, Jenkins. I've met very few fillies who don't end up lipping salt out of my hand."

The slick-haired back-easter opened his mouth to object, but an impatient Steele cut him off. "Never mind all that, Ambrose. Let's get down to cases, shall we?"

He rose from his desk and turned to a map of the New Mexico Territory on the wall behind him.

"The moment that stage rolls beyond the northern city limits of El Paso, you'll be in New Mexico. No Texas Rangers, no militia, no cavalry riding to the rescue. The garrison at Fort Union is barely adequate for post protection. It's this damned North-South conflict boiling up back east—federal troops are being called back from the frontier outposts."

All this was old news to Fargo. "Which means," he said, "that besides anything Lomax or whoever has in store, Apaches and freebooters can attack at will."

Steele nodded. "As far as terrain, this is not a particularly grueling run. You'll follow the fairly level Rio Grande Valley until you're well north of Albuquerque. At Cochiti Lake the stage road hooks due east into Santa Fe. Once you leave the valley and head east, terrain features become more of a hindrance—and a threat."

"Yeah, I've rode that stretch," Fargo said. "Heavily forested hills, some with steep grades."

"Precisely. And the Rio Grande Valley, while mostly level, has stretches of heavy forests such as Bosque Grande and the area around the Isleta Indian Reservation."

"The bosques," Fargo interjected. "In other words, plenty of good ambush country along much of the route. Is this stage a four-in-hand rig?"

Steele nodded. "Leaders and a wheel team are adequate for the valley portion. That's four big Cleveland bays, strong horses. At Cochiti Lake we add a swing team for the hills."

Fargo shook his head. "I want six horses for the entire run."

"But why? It's not—"

"The swing team," Fargo cut him off, "won't be for extra pulling. You both say you want this actress to get through. The easiest way to strand that coach is to kill a team horse or two. With a swing team in the middle, we'll have two replacements."

Steele looked annoyed at himself. "Good thinking, Fargo. And why not tie two more to the back of the coach along with your horse?"

Fargo's eyebrows almost touched when he frowned. "Now why would my stallion be tied off? I know I'm supposed to protect this woman, but riding inside the coach with her ain't the smart way to do it."

"You won't be inside—you'll be up on the box with the driver. You're replacing the regular shotgun rider."

"That's just hog stupid, Mr. Steele. Why lose the extra gun? And I'll need to scout out ahead—"

Steele raised one hand to silence him.

"Fargo, you underestimate your own notoriety. Plenty of our shotgun riders wear buckskins and beards, so up on the box, with your hat pulled low, you'll cause no undue notice. Likewise, with your Ovaro tied between two huge bays he won't stand out. But with you *on* that Ovaro, and riding separately, you'll be recognized."

Jenkins pitched in. "It's the same reason why I don't want a military escort, Fargo. We want this stagecoach as anonymous as possible."

"That's also why I discouraged Mr. Jenkins from using an extra coach," Steele said, meaning a special run not part of the published schedule. "Word gets out too quick on extras."

Fargo mulled it and finally nodded. "All that shines, I reckon."

Steele again pointed to the map. "We have another problem. You know, of course, that a stagecoach route is divided into stages of about ten to twelve miles by stations and swing stations. The swing stations provide fresh teams only; the stations are actually the homes of our station masters, where the passengers are fed and allowed to sleep."

"I see which way you're grazing," Fargo said. "Indian

raids and Mexican gangs have burned out some of the stations. I passed some of them on my way here—places like Mesquite, Rincon and Elephant Butte."

Steele nodded glumly. "Which means some of the stages have stretched out to thirty miles or more without relief. Fargo, under ideal trail conditions a Concord swift wagon with a fresh team can cut dirt at nine miles per hour. But seldom is any trail 'ideal' for very long. And I can't guarantee that even more stations won't be destroyed."

"Meaning," Fargo filled the ensuing pause for him, "that we just might find ourselves stranded with an exhausted team—and forced to camp on our own while fighting off assassins."

Jenkins looked perturbed at this intelligence, so neither Fargo nor Addison Steele mentioned what both men knew full well: even the stations that were still operating varied widely in quality. Some of the station masters—especially the Mexicans—placed great value on hospitality. Others, however, ranged from inhospitable to outright thieves who rifled passengers' luggage.

Some just *might* give up their own bedroom for a famous actress, Fargo realized. Others might force the great lady to eat weevil-infested food and sleep on the floor like a dog.

Jenkins searched both men's faces and didn't like what he read in them. He drew himself up in a huff. "Now see here, Steele—you didn't mention this lack of amenities to me during our first meeting. *Camping!* Sir, this is a great artiste, not some—"

"Things are the way they are, Jenkins. This isn't Manhattan or Paris. Frequent raiding, and the overall manpower shortage out west, forces us to make do—and sometimes to contract with unsavory elements."

"I see. But not to lower the exorbitant price of the fare. You—"

"Whack the cork," Fargo snapped impatiently. "Each Concord coach costs twelve hundred dollars, and they pay dear for horses, too. Unless your 'great artiste' can grow wings and fly to Santa Fe, she hasn't got much choice."

Fargo looked at Steele again. "What about her fellow passengers? Have you checked them out?"

"Insofar as I can, but I'm no Pinkerton man."

Steele rummaged in some papers on top of the desk until he located a passenger manifest. "There's four besides Miss Barton and I perceive none as a threat. There's one other woman—a pretty little thing who calls herself Trixie Belle. Claims she's a singer, but I suspect she's 'working her way west,' as they say."

"Sounds like your type, Fargo," Jenkins interjected spitefully.

"There's also," Steele went on, "an eccentric but utterly harmless little fellow named Malachi Feldman. Calls himself an 'astrological doctor' or some such foolishness. And an Episcopalian minister named Hinton Brandenburg. The fourth passenger is one Lansford Stratton, some type of businessman, I believe. Quite cultivated—keeps a silver snuffbox tucked up one sleeve. I figured he might be good company for Miss Barton."

"Depends what's tucked up the other sleeve," Fargo said, almost to himself.

"Fargo, I doubt—"

"Who's the driver?" Fargo cut him off.

"Well, of course we switch drivers about every sixty miles. I have some of our best reinsmen lined up."

Fargo shook his head. "We'll use one driver all the way. And I'll settle for no man but Booger McTeague."

Steele's eyes bulged like wet, white marbles. "Bill McTeague! And for the entire drive? Fargo, what is wrong with you and what doctor told you so?"

"No need to slip your traces. Can you name any other knight of the ribbons with a better record of getting his passengers delivered—or with fewer coach turnovers?"

"Well, I . . . no. No, he's a master whip and rarely rolls a coach. But, Fargo! With a great actress aboard? Why, he—"

Fargo waved him silent. "Yeah, I know. He's one of those men who talks a lot without thinking it out first. Booger is a foulmouthed, hard-drinking, foul-smelling heathen, and half crazy into the deal. He once made my horse blush, and he could send Satan screaming from hell. Just the man I want for this job."

"Foulmouthed?" Jenkins echoed. "A heathen? Now see

here, Fargo. Kathleen Barton attended finishing school in Paris, her father is ambassador to—"

"I don't care if her old man squires the Queen of England. Do you want her alive in Santa Fe or dead in a nameless grave?" Fargo demanded. "It's Booger McTeague or I'm dusting my hocks right now."

Jenkins purpled but clamped his mouth shut. Steele sighed, then suddenly flashed a little grin at the bizarre irony of it. Bill "Booger" McTeague and Kathleen Barton sharing the same stagecoach—and Skye Fargo the instigator of it. God in whirlwinds! If a bullet didn't cut Fargo down, those two surely would.

"Well, then, Fargo, if you insist."

Steele wore a double-breasted waistcoat with wide lapels. He reached inside it and removed a watch from the fob pocket of his vest, thumbing back the cover. "That means I'll have to hunt him down, and there's twenty-seven saloons in El Paso, not to mention all the cathouses. I'll try to have him sober by departure time tomorrow morning."

"Getting him sober is a lost cause," Fargo said. "Just tell him Skye Fargo wants to help him get killed. I guarantee that'll fetch him."

3

The sun had still not cleared the adobe-pocked hilltops of El Paso by the time Skye Fargo rode into the big side yard of Overland's depot. As he swung down from the saddle and tossed the reins forward, a young Mexican boy hustled to meet him.

"Que caballo tan grande!" the *mozo* exclaimed, admiring Fargo's black-and-white stallion. "Such a fine horse, Senor Fargo!"

"He ain't the worst nag around," the Trailsman allowed, and the Ovaro's tail suddenly slapped Fargo's face.

"Caramba! Your horse, he understands American?"

"Oh, he knows a little Spanish, too. But he can't cipher worth a damn."

The *mozo* pointed toward a front corner of the adobe depot. "The coach, she is ready. Everything as you ordered, senor."

Even Fargo, no friend of western progress, could not help admiring the fine conveyance, built by the Abbot-Downing Company of Concord, New Hampshire, and exported worldwide. Its wooden wheels, nearly indestructible, and powerful brake mechanism made it highly reliable for travel on the frontier. It was also a visual work of art: the coach was painted a highly varnished black with gold striping; the wheels, axles, springs and shafts were emerald green.

The most passenger-friendly feature, however, were the thick leather straps—thoroughbraces—upon which the body was suspended. On rough and washboard trails, passengers were not flung violently around, injuring knees and elbows. Instead, the body of the coach swung fore and aft like a rocking chair.

"Here, kid." Fargo flipped the *mozo* two bits. "Water my horse good, wouldja? Then strip all the leather and toss it on top the Concord rig. Be careful of the rifle in my saddle boot—it's a Henry and the tube magazine bends easy."

"*Claro*, senor!"

Fargo headed toward the depot, calling over his shoulder: "When he's finished drinking, tie him off between those two bays behind the coach."

"*'Sta bien,* senor."

The Ovaro, like Fargo, did not like close herding, but the big Cleveland bay was famous for tenacious strength and a gentle disposition. And stallions were generally tolerant of geldings. If this trip proved as dangerous as Addison Steele and Ambrose Jenkins feared it would, Fargo wanted his horse safe between two even bigger horses.

El Paso was a busy stagecoach hub and Fargo found the passenger waiting area already surprisingly busy. Passengers were grouped on long benches by route and departure time, and he spotted Steele standing near four seated passengers, politely chatting. When he saw Fargo enter, he stepped discreetly away to greet him.

"I finally located Bill McTeague last night," he told Fargo. "He was at Rosie's Cantina, goading men to punch him in the face for the price of a jolt glass of whiskey."

Fargo grinned. "He's alla time inviting men to give him a 'facer.' They always decline and buy him a drink anyway because he scares the hell out of them."

Steele visibly shuddered. "He's not a man—he's a nation. Would *you* punch him in the face even by invitation?"

"I druther grab a grizzly by the nuts. So, will he be whipping the stage?"

"Surely you jest? The moment he heard your name he picked me up and twirled me around the floor until I was dizzy. Swore he'd get you killed this time. My ribs still ache from the hug he gave me."

Steele frowned as he thought of something else. "Normally this run to Santa Fe would include a conductor to see to the passengers' safety and comfort—that's especially important when such a prominent woman as Kathleen Barton is among the passengers. But the only two conductors I

15

presently have available refuse to ride with McTeague. One swears he is a cannibal and the other claims he is an inveterate bully."

"Oh, he's a bully," Fargo agreed, "and *I* wouldn't walk in front of him during starving times. But according to Booger, he never eats a friend."

Steele studied Fargo's deadpan face, trying to decide if that was a joke. "I see," he said awkwardly.

Fargo turned his attention to the four passengers. "No sign of the great lady yet, hey?"

"Oh, there's one sign of her," Steele replied ruefully, pointing to a huge stack of expensive leather trunks beside the door. "That stack could never fit in the boot. Twenty-five pounds is Overland's recommended limit. We enforce that limit by charging a whopping dollar a pound for excess weight, but she paid it without blinking. Fortunately, the male passengers are traveling light."

"Those trunks are good," Fargo approved. "We'll strap 'em topside with the mail sacks. It may put a few bullet holes in her dainties, but I favor the idea of a breastwork up there in case of ambushes."

"Speaking of bullet holes . . . I know you're loyal to that Henry repeater of yours, but you can't play the part of a shotgun rider without a shotgun. There's a double-ten express gun for you up on the box. Careful with it—it kicks like a Missouri mule."

Fargo was still studying the waiting passengers. The young woman calling herself Trixie Belle had been slanting approving glances toward Fargo since he'd walked in. Now, seeing him watch her, she sent him a sexy up-and-under look, batting her long lashes.

Steele snorted. "Looks like you've made your first conquest, Fargo. Pretty little thing, isn't she?"

"Mighty easy on the eyes," Fargo agreed. "Dressed a bit gaudy for traveling, though."

Hooped petticoats were currently all the rage among American women but strictly forbidden by all stage lines—some crinoline cages occupied an entire seat, and a careless cigar ash could set a woman ablaze in mere moments. Trixie Belle wore a form-hugging, feather-trimmed gown whose bold décolletage and tight stays bared at least half of her breasts. She had a pleasing oval face, with sea-green eyes, under a profusion of golden ringlets.

"I can't decide if she's a soiled dove or just a dime-a-dance gal," Steele said. "Or maybe she really is a singer. But she's certainly no hired killer, eh?"

"I'd say she's perfect for that job," Fargo gainsaid. "A man gazing at those tits wouldn't even see it coming. Think I'll introduce myself to the passengers."

Even before Fargo stopped in front of Trixie, the petite woman came excitedly to her feet. "My stars and garters! I've seen your handsome likeness in *Frontier Adventures*. You're Skye Fargo, ain'tcha?"

Fargo had expected to be recognized sooner or later thanks to the penny dreadfuls and shilling shockers. He touched the brim of his hat. "Miss, they'd sell more copies with *your* likeness on the cover."

She blushed prettily. "Why, how gallant! My name is Trixie Belle. Well, actually, it's Priscilla Urbanski when I'm back home in Cleveland. But that name won't do for a thirst-parlor singer. I'm hoping to get on in Santa Fe, you see. Will you be riding the coach with us, Mr. Fargo?"

"In a manner of speaking, Trixie. I'll be riding shotgun."

The other three passengers—all men—had looked startled when Trixie pronounced Fargo's name. Now a long-faced, narrow-shouldered man dressed in clergy black and a battered homburg, clutching a big clasp Bible, spoke up.

"Mr. Fargo, Pastor Brandenburg here. I, too, have heard something of your . . . violent exploits. Isn't this rather menial work for a man of your reputation?"

Fargo's lake blue eyes, direct as searchlights, quickly took the clergyman's measure. He was whipcord thin and gifted with a sonorous baritone voice that should have compelled respect. But his ridiculously long, hanging sideburns—known back East as Picadilly Weepers—made him a ludicrous figure in Fargo's eyes.

"I was headed to Santa Fe anyway," Fargo lied, "so I figured I might's well profit from the trip."

"Now, now, Mr. Fargo," broke in an unkempt, plump man of indeterminate middle age sitting next to the preacher. He wore gray homespun and battered brogans. "I can tell, from the ectoplasmic aura surrounding you, that you are prevaricating with us."

Fargo grinned. "Now, *that* was a string of thirty-five cent words. You must be Malachi Feldman, astrological doctor."

"I am indeed, sir. Doctor Malachi Feldman, possessor of the Third Eye that sees hidden truth. I merely said—and I intend no offense—that you are not being truthful. Probably, however, for noble reasons. By nature you are an honest man."

"And you figured that out from my ecto-whosis?"

"Your ectoplasmic aura, sir. Every human being is surrounded by a thin radiance visible to us who possess the Third Eye. Yours was a normal blue radiance until you answered the pastor's question—then it suddenly shaded over into red as you told your fib."

"I take plenty of guff from my friends, but usually I won't tolerate a stranger calling me a liar. But since you called me a noble liar, I reckon I'll overlook it."

Fargo retained his amused mask, but inwardly he was taken aback. He had indeed been lying, of course, but how could this blather-spouting jasper have known?

A harsh bark of laughter from the fourth passenger on the bench diverted Fargo's attention.

"I'd call that a genuine bug of the genus 'hum,'" proclaimed the big, hard-knit man who must be Lansford Ashton. He had a bluff, weather-seamed face, shrewd eyes, and a thin line of mustache with a pointed Vandyke beard. He wore an immaculate white linen suit with a silver concho belt. He spoke in the dusty drawl of the West Texas chaparral country.

"Don't let this fat little grifter honey-fuggle you, Fargo," he added. "You might say he's less than meets the eye. Look at those fancy trunks piled up by the door. Moroccan leather with gold studs. Obviously someone of immense wealth, and likely immense importance, will be riding to Santa Fe with us. Add to the mix a gent of your caliber as lowly shotgun rider and the conclusion is as obvious as clown makeup: you've secretly been hired as a bodyguard. 'Third Eye' my sweet aunt."

"The secret would've come out soon enough," Fargo said

amiably while Malachi Feldman shot Ashton a poisonous glance. ''But I commend your powers of observation, friend.''

''Lansford Ashton, Mr. Fargo, businessman's agent by profession. You might say that I specialize in clearing potential profit paths of all that encumbers them—legally, when possible, artfully when not. I've recently been engaged by a consortium of Santa Fe silver miners who are far more ambitious than clever.''

''Based on my first impression of you, Mr. Ashton, I predict they'll soon be thriving. You don't strike me as a man who does things by halves.''

Ashton opened his mouth to reply, but just then the depot exploded with boom-claps of thunder in the form of spoken words. ''Skye goldang Fargo, you horny son of trouble! Come give Booger a kiss!''

As he turned slowly around Fargo experienced an involuntary shudder and took in a deep breath, for he knew only too well what was coming next.

The moonfaced man beaming at Fargo was a virtual man-mountain who canceled the daylight behind him as he stepped into the depot doorway. Standing six foot five inches tall and weighing two hundred and eighty-five pounds, Bill ''Booger'' McTeague crossed the large distance in a few lumbering strides, opening his arms wide and bearing down on Fargo like the Apocalypse.

Fargo felt the air crushed from his lungs when Booger swept him up like a sack of feathers, giving him a bear hug that would have killed a Quaker.

''Skye Fargo, you sheep-humping, chicken-plucking bastard of the sage, many is the night I've prayed you into the ground! Ain't seen you since Christ was a corporal! Why, lad, it's been five long years since we stood back to back and created Comanche widows and orphans at Antelope Wells!''

The shaggy giant finally set Fargo down just before the Trailsman blacked out from lack of oxygen. Booger was thick in the chest and waist, his arms bigger around the wrist than most brawny men were in the forearms. He wore a floppy hat and butternut-dyed shirt and trousers with knee-length elk-skin moccasins.

''Faugh! The sun has peeped up and no liquor on your

breath? You and your barley pop'—'beer and draw it nappy.'
By God, you son of a motherless goat, you'll learn to drink
tiger spit like a man when you side old Booger!'

The impressive reinsman forced a glass flask into Fargo's
hands. Fargo knew he had no choice in the matter and
knocked back a slug. It was the savage brew known as Taos
Lightning, and immediately filmed his eyes.

'Why, you titty baby!' Booger mocked him in his back-
water twang. 'I—' Booger suddenly caught sight of Trixie
Belle, who was gaping as if he were a talking elephant. His
eyes widened at the sight of her generous bosoms.

'Crikes, what gorgeous jahoobies!' he exclaimed. 'Fargo,
have you showed her your trouser snake yet? It's a square
deal started by Eve: one angry serpent for those two juicy
apples.'

'Why, God bless me, sir!' protested the preacher, his sal-
low face now pale. 'You carry a pang to my heart with such
barbarous blasphemy. Please launder your vulgar speech in
front of ladies and a man of God.'

Booger squinted at his horrified passenger. 'No Choctaw
here, catfish. So I've panged you, have I? A man of God, eh?
Well, I'm the favorite son of Satan, and soon there'll be a hot
pitchfork in your ass if you don't put a stopper on your gob,
holy man. I've no use for the drizzling shits nor witch doc-
tors. Me and Fargo ain't been Bible-raised, so chuck the
mealymouthed sermons or sing your death song.'

'Ahem!' Addison Steele cleared his throat nervously and
cast an I-told-you-so look at Fargo. Trixie and the astrological doctor were frozen in shock. Lansford Ashton, however,
Fargo noticed, seemed to be enjoying this farce immensely.

'Bill,' Steele suggested, 'perhaps we should start boarding the passengers now. And there are trunks to strap down
on the roof of the coach. Also, Fargo will want to go outside
with you and fill you in on some details.'

'We seem to be one passenger short,' Ashton remarked.
'Certainly we cannot leave without our important personage?'

Fargo eyed the coolly confident man speculatively. But as
if Ashton were a herald, Ambrose Jenkins stepped into the
depot with a stunningly beautiful woman on his arm—one
so stunning that the depot went as silent as a classroom after

a hard question. Even Booger McTeague was struck speechless, a rare event.

It was Ashton who broke the silence. "As I live and breathe—that fairest flower of all the fields, ladies and gentlemen, is Kathleen Barton, America's Sweetheart."

About one hundred yards north of the Overland Stage line's El Paso depot, Cleo Hastings knelt before a fourth-story window in the Frontier Hotel. The notch sight of his Sharps carbine was centered on Skye Fargo's back.

"God-*damn* it, Russ! I'm telling you, man, I can pop Fargo over right *now*! *Now*, buddy, before he even climbs up onto that box. That's our job, ain't it? Just one twitch, Russ, and he's bucked out."

Russ Alcott and Spider Winslowe sat at a table cutting cards for a dime a go. Alcott glanced toward the window and shook his head in disgust.

"Cleo, you dumb cockchafer, you ain't got the brains God gave a pissant. Pull that smoke pole in before somebody spots it."

"But why, damn it!" Cleo looked back over his right shoulder, his face imploring. He was a thickset man with a huge soup-strainer mustache and a pockmarked face. "You think I can't make the shot, hanh?"

Alcott kept his voice level only with an effort. "Now see, this here is why I'm the wheel and you're just a pip-squeak cog. Sure, my damn grandmother could make that shot. But I told you to pull that rifle back inside, and I don't chew my cabbage twice."

"Like hell I will! We kill him now and it's did. Lomax pays us the rest of our money, and we ain't gotta lock horns with Fargo up the trail. I'm popping that son of a bitch over *now*."

Cleo was still curling his finger around the trigger when two menacing, metallic clicks behind him raised the fine hairs on his nape. He looked around and stared into the unblinking eyes of Russ' and Spider's six-guns.

"Go ahead and pull that trigger," Alcott said in a voice dry as husks scraping in an old cornfield. "Pull it, and you'll buck out a second after Fargo."

Cleo, looking as if he'd been drained by leeches, slowly pulled his carbine inside and laid it on the plank floor.

"Cleo," Russ said as if talking to a child, "a man don't wade into the water until he knows how deep it is. Now you tell me—what happens as soon as you kill Fargo in that wagon yard? What happens to the bitch before you can get another cap on that nib and get back on bead?"

"She . . . why, I reckon they'd hustle her back inside, huh?"

"Atta boy, now you're whistling. And after she sees Fargo's guts fly out all over her pretty dress, you think she'll hop on that coach and just head north, pretty as you please?"

Hastings thought about it, then shook his head. "Nah. She might never go to Santa Fe at all. And then Lomax don't pay us."

"That ain't all, jughead," Spider cut in. He had thinning red hair and a crooked nose broken in two places. "You see that wooden barracks just past the feed store? Texas Ranger headquarters. You got any idea how them old boys feel about Skye Fargo?"

"And the New Mexico Territory," Alcott added, flipping over an ace of spades, "allows hot pursuit for crimes committed in Texas. No matter which way we run, they'll be pouring hot lead up our bung holes."

By now Cleo was thoroughly chastised. "Yeah. I didn't think about none a that shit."

"You don't need to think, Cleo," Alcott assured him, quickly building a smoke and expertly curling the ends. "You got enough guts to fill a smokehouse, and you can shoot the eyes out of a crow at two hundred yards. You're a damn good man to take along, and that's why you're here. As for Skye Fargo and Lomax's silky-satin bitch"—Alcott's cruelly handsome face set itself hard—"I got a real nice plan worked out for them. Fargo ain't never seen me, so I'll be waiting for them at the Vado station. I want to get a good size-up of this galoot and see if I can puzzle out which passenger is on Lomax's payroll."

"I don't like that shit," Cleo declared. "I mean, Lomax not telling us who he hired."

"It don't set good with me, neither. But this deal has got

to be done right—from what I hear about Fargo, one mistake can be our epitaph."

"My pap was a coffin maker," Spider put in. "Every time I cut a board for him, he told me to measure it twice and cut it once."

Alcott tossed his head back and blew three perfect smoke rings toward the ceiling. Then he trained his pale-ice eyes on Spider and nodded.

"Your pap was a smart man, and that's how we're gonna work this deal. Just remember this: If we want the top money, *we* got to kill Fargo and not let it fall to whoever Lomax has hired to ride the stage. His main job is to keep the actress on the coach until Lomax douses her glims farther north. But we have to do for Fargo first or that ain't never gonna happen."

4

Fargo, Booger and the *mozo* made short work of securing
Kathleen Barton's trunks to the flat top of the Concord.
Fargo was just tying the last hitch knot when Addison Steele
led the boarding party out into the yard.

"Ha-ho, ha-ho," Booger said, eyeing the actress. "*There's*
one petticoat you won't get under, Tumbledown Dick. You
seen that look she give you when Steele innerduced you to
her? Christmas crackers! Like you ain't good 'nuff to lick
her silk boots."

"I'm generally better at unlacing than lacing," Fargo
assured the shaggy giant.

"Pah! *That* one pisses icicles. You can't jump a four-rail
fence, Trailsman."

"The cat sits patiently by the gopher hole," Fargo said as
he began clambering down.

Fargo had heard and read about Kathleen Barton's famed
beauty but had never seen a likeness of her. Watching her
approach now, proudly holding separate from the rest of the
chattering passengers, he understood the widespread claim
that she was the most beautiful woman in America. Her
wing-shaped, amber-brown eyes and regal, arching eyebrows set off a beautifully symmetrical face. The thick,
coffee-colored hair was swept back tight under a jewel-
encrusted tiara. Her complexion was like creamy lotion, and
the delicate, disdainful lips matched her icy hauteur.

But Fargo realized the "wide-eyed vivacity" theater crit-
ics claimed she projected on stage was nowhere evident
now—just a cool disdain for all the lesser mortals around
her. But great jumping Judas, he told himself, that woman
makes Venus look like a dishrag.

Her melodic but stern voice slapped him out of his reverie. "You do realize, Mr. Fargo, that men can also grope with their eyes?"

Booger sniggered and whispered, "Looks like gopher hole is *all* you'll get, chappie."

Fargo touched his hat. "It was more in the way of admiring a great painting, Miss Barton, not groping. You're mighty easy on the eyes, and you can't hang a man for his thoughts."

She ignored that. "No offense to your *manly pride*, Mr. Fargo, but I consider your presence on this journey superfluous."

"Now, now, Kathleen," Ambrose Jenkins tried to soothe his client, "you yourself showed me the anonymous letter. You also told me you believe it was sent by Zack Lomax, whom you believe is still alive."

"All that is true and the man's very name is gall and wormwood to me. But you see"—here she turned to Fargo again—"I believe strongly in Fate. Whatever may happen, Mr. Fargo, is out of your no-doubt roughly callused hands."

"I believe in Fate, too," Fargo said. "Fate is the hand you are dealt, the cards you can't choose yourself. But Fate also allows for discards and the skill of the player."

For a moment she looked surprised, even perhaps a bit impressed. "My stars, a buckskin-clad philosopher? What's next—the sun rising in the west?"

"I agree with Fargo, Miss Barton," Lansford Ashton put in politely. "And all due respect, but I would never judge a man of his capabilities superfluous. As the Latin phrase goes, *vestis virum reddit*—'the clothes make the man.' And buckskin is very tough indeed."

Hearing his perfect Latin, she glanced at Ashton with some interest. But Malachi Feldman now spoke up eagerly. "You are certainly correct, Miss Barton—our fate is predetermined and in the stars and planets, not the hands of Fargo. If you will kindly tell me which astrological sign you were born under, I—"

"Pitch it to hell, pip-squeak," Booger cut in impatiently. "It's time to cut dirt, not listen to your swamp gas. All aboard!"

Steele and Jenkins handed the ladies in. Booger stared eagerly at the ivory swell of Trixie Belle's boldly exposed bosoms.

"Her Nibs and Her Nips," he whispered in the Trailsman's ear. "Fargo, lad, our cornucopia runneth over. *Both* them little bits of frippet put a pup tent in my britches. And I know exactly where and how we are going to view both them gals buck naked."

Fargo started to ask for details, but Booger waved him off. "You will see, lad. Old Booger has his little tricks."

The come-hither glance Trixie sent Fargo, as she stepped into the coach, convinced him he'd be seeing at least this woman naked—assuming a load of blue whistlers didn't cancel his plans.

The sturdy coach listed to one side as Booger heaved himself up on the box. He slid on the buckskin gauntlets that no true knight of the ribbons would be caught without. Then he pulled a six-horse whip from its socket: the buckskin lash was twenty feet long and able to reach the leaders of a three-team rig. Fargo ducked behind the coach to check on the Ovaro. The stallion's lazy tail was swishing at flies, and he had evidently accepted the close proximity of the gentle bays.

"Fargo!" Booger hollered. "Sling your hook or you'll be eating dust! I've no patience with a malt worm who puts water after his whiskey."

Fargo, the double-ten in one hand, barely had his foot on the steel rung before Booger cracked his blacksnake and the coach lurched into motion with a jangle of trace chains.

"Gerlong there, boys! G'long! *Whoop!*"

Something in the tail of his eye made Fargo glance toward the five-story hotel on his right. A man's face stared out a fourth-floor window at him but quickly ducked out of sight.

"Interesting," Fargo muttered, making sure his brass-framed Henry was conveniently to hand behind him. An express gun was formidable indeed, at close range, but Fargo suspected his sixteen-shot Henry might soon prove more useful.

Booger was in high spirits at seeing his old battle companion again.

"Ahh, the morning-crisp glory of the sun, eh, Fargo? Watch this."

Booger stared into the bright yellow ball of sun until he sneezed so violently the wheel team pricked up their ears.

"Works every time! If I aim my ass at old Sol, might be I'll cut a fart, hey?"

"Let's just go on wondering," Fargo suggested as they rolled through the northern outskirts of El Paso, his eyes constantly scanning to all sides. "Booger, did anything I told you back at the depot sink in?"

"What? About this Lomax wanting to kill the Ice Queen? Faugh! Can you blame him? *That* calico is all horns and rattles."

"Tell the truth and shame the devil. But don't forget—it's likely *we'll* be the first targets. And I'd wager we're being watched already. I think maybe I spotted one of the killers as we pulled out of the depot. It's also highly likely they'll wait until we're deeper into New Mexico."

Booger snorted. "Ahh, go crap in your hat, malt worm. Why, this run will be like money for old rope. I've survived Comanches, Apaches, Kiowas, the French Pox and two years of bloody war down in Old Mex."

He gnawed off a corner of his plug, got it juicing good, then cheeked his cud and let out a dramatic sigh.

"Yes, lad, the war. Blood, guts, senseless slaughter, terrible suffering and treachery, unmitigated human misery— oh, Skye, I do miss it! Life has gone to hell for old Booger, it has. Where the grapeshot is pouring in, that's where I long to be. Hee-*yah*, you spavined whores!" he added, cracking his whip over the leaders.

"*Please*, Mr. McTeague!" the preacher shouted through one of the windows. "The ladies can hear you!"

Booger grinned malevolently. "That prissy holy man wears cologne in them droopy side whiskers. You get within four feet of that rake handle and your eyeballs mist."

"Never mind him. Wha'd'ya think about Lansford Ashton?"

The mirth bled from Booger's moon face. "Aye, there's a weasel dick and an oily tongue. He spoke up for you to the actress, but it was only lip deep. Bad medicine. Are you thinking he's hired by Lomax—that Lomax knows the very rig Her Nibs is riding?"

"That's two good questions," Fargo pointed out, "but I've got no good answers. I think it's smart to assume Lomax knows which coach and that he's planted somebody on it. But consider all those passengers potential killers, not just Ashton."

"Even Trixie? She of the giant jahoobies?"

"Even her."

Booger nodded and loosed a brown streamer that splatted on the withers of the offside wheeler. "All right, catfish. But if it's her, let's make damn sure we screw her before we kill her."

The first stage of the journey into New Mexico Territory went off without a hitch. The stage rolled through the narrow but fertile Rio Grande Valley, green with well-cultivated fields of beans, squash and chili peppers.

Fargo could see the river on his left, a wide, meandering brown ribbon still high with spring runoff from the northern mountains. On his right, the fertile fields gave way like a knife edge to yellow-brown desert. Beyond this desolate vista, the Organ Mountains cut dark silhouettes against a cloudless sky of bottomless blue. Mountains seldom seemed close in New Mexico, yet they always saw-toothed the horizons.

The day heated up quickly as the morning advanced, and Fargo was soon mopping his forehead with his sleeve. They changed teams at the Berino swing station. When Fargo hopped down and glanced into the coach, he had to stifle a grin—Kathleen Barton alone occupied the leather-padded seat at the rear, cut off from the other four passengers.

"Mr. Fargo," Pastor Brandenburg complained out the window, "you really *must* speak to that driver! Those filthy songs he bellows out, and his coarse language—why, the ladies are positively scandalized!"

"I think he's funny," Trixie contradicted, pouring out a smile for Fargo. "I liked that ditty about granny swinging on the outhouse door without her nightgown."

"Tell you what, Preacher," Fargo said from a deadpan, pointing to the other side of the coach. "There's Booger now—speak to him yourself."

The man of God followed Fargo's finger, his face contorting into a horrified mask: Booger McTeague stood in open view, pissing into the sand.

"God preserve us," the preacher muttered.

Booger saw the rest staring. "Why, a man must drain his snake, hey? It's two more hours before we reach the station at Vado. If anyone needs to piss, best let 'er rip now!"

Lansford Ashton met Fargo's gaze. "Earthy fellow, isn't he?"

Kathleen Barton deigned to break her demure silence, those bewitching amber-brown eyes staring at Fargo as she spoke. "You mustn't confuse earth with dirt, Mr. Lansford."

Fargo grinned, touched his hat, then lent the stock-tender a hand with the new relay before they rolled on again. The open, cultivated terrain so far set Fargo somewhat at ease. Occasionally they encountered serape-draped *indios* and Mexicans, afoot, on burros or riding in carts pulled by donkeys, and Fargo kept a wary eye on them until they were out of sight.

"Money for old rope," Booger insisted again after tipping his flask and passing it to Fargo. "The Ice Queen is safe as sassafras. We may have to kill a few stray road agents or Apaches is all."

Booger's North & Savage rifle protruded from a leather boot at the corner of the box, and his old cap-and-ball dragoon pistol from the Mexican War was tucked behind his red sash. Fargo knew firsthand that he was a dead shot with both weapons.

"Like I said," Fargo reminded him, "the trouble is likely to come farther north where it's good ambush country."

"Fargo, you've become a reg'lar calamity howler. You eat too much pussy—such a diet renders a man feminine. Say, here's a lulu! There's this jasper riding a train from Cincinnati to Chicago, you see, and all of a sudden like he's got to take him a powerful shit. Just then the train whooshes into a tunnel, and in the dark he drops his britches and hangs his ass out a window.

"Well, sir, there's these two bummers camped in the tunnel beside the tracks. One of 'em looks up, all excited like: 'Look-a-there, Pete, see that? Quick, man! You slap his face and I'll grab the cigar!' "

Booger found his own joke so amusing he laughed himself into a coughing fit, shaking the entire coach. "Ain't that the berries, Skye? See, he thought—"

"Yeah, I *grasp* it," Fargo punned, and when Booger got his play on words he almost rolled off the box in new paroxysms of mirth.

"But if it was dark inside the tunnel," Trixie's voice called up to them, "how could they see the—"

"Ignore them, young lady," the preacher's voice snapped, raised for Booger's enlightenment. "You must resist corrupting influences, not encourage them."

Booger winked at Fargo. "The game's afoot, lad. The witch doctor is my favorite boy now. Oh, great larks ahead!"

Early in the afternoon they rolled into the Overland station house at Vado, a low cottonwood structure chinked with mud. A fresh relay team waited in the hoof-packed side yard.

Many way stations also sold food and liquor to passersby. Fargo spotted a lone roan gelding, still saddled, hitched to the snorting post out front.

"That's fine horseflesh," he remarked as Booger kicked the brake handle. "But sore-used. See the scars where it's been spurred in the shoulders? Spurred hard."

"Outlaw horse," Booger said. "Sure as cats fighting."

Fargo nodded. "Hold the passengers out here a minute while I talk to the *mozo*. I want me and you stepping inside first."

Fargo instructed the yard boy to untie the three horses from the back of the Concord and let them tank up at the stone water trough.

"Any trouble inside?" he asked the Mexican kid.

The lad shrugged and removed his straw Chihuahua hat in a mark of respect. *"No hable ingles, senor."*

"Hay un hombre malo dentro de la casa?"

"There is one stranger," the kid replied in Spanish. "He ate a bowl of pozole and now he is drinking whiskey. He has been very quiet. There has been no trouble."

Fargo thanked him and sent a high sign to Booger, who flung open the doors of the coach. While the preacher and Ashton handed out the ladies, Fargo and Booger went ahead into the station master's home, Fargo knocking the riding thong off the hammer of his Colt.

The large front room was simple and clean, with a white-washed clay floor and a long trestle table with two wooden benches. *Ristras*, bunches of dried red chili peppers, hung from the low ceiling. The place smelled wonderfully of beef and green-chili stew. In the far front corner was a short plank bar. A shelf on the wall behind it held a few bottles of whiskey and the milky cactus liquor called pulque.

But it was the lone figure slouched over the bar who focused Fargo's attention. His lean profile was handsome but mean, and his fancy star-roweled spurs of Mexican silver were mean, too—the rowels sharpened to vicious points for brutal domination of a horse. In this vast and lawless territory Fargo was used to encountering rough, unshaven fellows with poor manners. This man, however, was well groomed and nodded politely at the new arrivals.

"Glom his two-gun rig," Booger muttered.

But Fargo already had. The hand-tooled holsters had been partly cut away, and the notches on the hammers of his wooden-gripped Colt Navy revolvers had been filed off to ensure the weapons wouldn't snag—a favorite trick of quick-draw artists. And rare was the honest man out West who wore two guns.

"Bad medicine," Booger added, but just then the smiling station master hustled forward to greet the new arrivals.

"Senor Booger!" he exclaimed. "I did not expect you today. Shall I butcher a cow?"

"I'll just eat it on the hoof, Pablo," the whip shot back.

A woman in a dark *rebozo*, who appeared to be Pablo's wife, fluttered about the passengers, getting them seated at the long table. Pottery cups and a pitcher of lemonade had already been set in place. The two Mexicans got a closer look at Kathleen Barton, and the *gringa*'s astonishing beauty left both of them slack-jawed.

"Looks like you're being groped again, Miss Barton," Fargo quipped.

She coolly ignored him, seating herself at some distance from the rest of the passengers. Fargo kept a careful, constant eye on the gunslick at the bar, who seemed to be carefully avoiding looking in their direction. Too carefully . . .

"Miss Barton," Trixie spoke up while Pablo's wife hustled back toward the kitchen. "I'm proud to say that the two of us are sorta in the same profession. You see, I'm a singer. I've been hired to sing at the La Paloma in Santa Fe."

"Oh? Is that a theater?"

"Well . . . it's a very fancy thirst parlor."

The actress peeled off her long silk gloves. "I thought so. I hardly think that being pawed in barrel houses, dance halls and gin mills—and no doubt bordellos—places you in my profession," she enunciated with punishing clarity.

Fargo watched Trixie flush deep to her earlobes. Booger grinned and winked at Fargo. *"R-r-r-i-i-n-n-n!"* he said in a bad imitation of a cat growling.

"I'm no scrubbed angel," Trixie admitted. "But you needn't treat me like the town pump, neither! Leastways, I ain't so hateful that I buy extra tickets so's I won't have to sit next to nobody."

"Here's a corset with starch in it," Booger approved.

"I'm sure you'd have to raise your rates to afford extra tickets," the disdainful thespian responded.

Trixie assumed a war face and started up from the bench, but Ashton gently tugged her back down. The preacher's watery nose made him sniff constantly. He did so now. "Ladies, this is unseemly in your gender. Such—"

"Pipe down, you jay, or I'll baste your bacon!" Booger snapped. "Every red-blooded man with a set on him dearly loves a good catfight. They may claw each other naked."

This was all good entertainment, but Fargo paid it scant attention. The gun-thrower across the room, he was nearly convinced by now, was not there by happenchance. It was time to take the bull by the horns. He pushed away from the table and strolled over to the bar.

"Something's got me a mite curious," Fargo greeted him without any polite preamble.

Ice-chip eyes raked quickly over Fargo. "Do tell? And just what might that be?"

"Men outnumber women about two hundred to one in these parts. Even a homely-lonely with buckteeth draws plenty of stares. Yet, right now at that table over there sit two prime specimens of female flesh. And you haven't craned your neck around once to look them over. Something's not jake with that."

"Tell you what. If you graze near a point, feel free as all hell to make it."

"It's been made."

"So you're telling me you're offended on account I ain't eye-fucking your women?"

"If that's how you want to play it, all right. Yeah—I'm offended."

Both men knew what it meant to "offend" a man in the Territories. The gunslick decided on a staring contest and soon regretted it. The carved-in-granite face staring back at him was as emotionless and lethal as a cocked rifle. The blue eyes that women found charming had the opposite effect on men: they bespoke implacable will and unshakable courage, and the wordless confidence of a man for whom killing was an instinct born of necessity.

The pale eyes slid away from his. "Look, mister, I got no dicker with you. I just come in here to have a couple quiet bracers and move on. You wonder why I ain't staring at them two beauties? Well, take a good gander at that mammoth ape sittin' with 'em. Just the sight of that big son of a bitch turns my liver white, and I admit it. *He* might be offended if I do look, and that's one farmer's bull I ain't looking to shake a red rag at."

The answer surprised Fargo. He didn't believe it for a moment, but it was highly logical and gave Fargo no more room to push. He did take a gander at Booger and realized he'd rather offend a den of rattlesnakes. Fargo, despite his suspicion, decided to ease off.

He planked two bits on the bar. "Have one on me."

He was on his way back to the table when the man said behind him, "Thank you, sir."

That servile word "sir" tore it for Fargo. There wasn't an ounce of humility in that snake-eyed killer, and more than one human maggot had called Fargo "sir" before trying to perforate his liver. This gunman was on Zack Lomax's payroll, and he knew damn well he had to murder Fargo to get at the real prize.

"Well," Kathleen Barton barbed as he arrived back at the table. "Do you feel better now that you've bullied a stranger who was only minding his own business?"

"And how do you feel," Fargo retorted, "after calling a friendly young woman a whore without knowing one damn thing about her?"

The unexpected parry struck the actress full force. "I—" She faltered and took a deep breath, looking at Trixie. "It pains me to say it, but Mr. Fargo is right. Miss Belle, I apologize for my harsh remarks."

Trixie, clearly not one to hold a grudge, smiled sweetly. "That's all right, Miss Barton. You're a great artist, and everybody knows great artists are temperamental. Heck, I *am* just a saloon singer."

Pastor Brandenburg beamed. "*That's* the Christian spirit, ladies. To err is human, to forgive—"

"Oh, caulk up, you mealymouthed peckerwood!" Booger exploded. He turned his murderous stare on the Trailsman. "What's got into you, Fargo—religion? We had us a jim-dandy catfight brewing up, and *you* just put the kibosh on it. Damn your sanctimonious bones to hell!"

5

"Boys," Russ Alcott declared solemnly, "I looked straight into that lanky son of a bitch's eyes. And I'm here to tell you—it was like staring right into the fiery pit. Skye Fargo is all he's cracked up to be and ten times more. I like to shit when I realized that buckskin bastard *knew* why I was there."

Alcott, Cleo Hastings and Spider Winslowe sat their saddles in a little cottonwood thicket beside the Rio Grande. Behind them, a westering sun gold-leafed the normally muddy river. Due east, across the green valley floor, the Overland stagecoach sent up a yellow plume of dust.

"Really gave you the fantods, huh?" Spider pressed.

Alcott's lips formed a tight seam. "Look here . . . I've killed eleven men in Lincoln County alone, and the bullets was all in the front. A few of them men I done for was some of the hardest hard cases you ever seen—men like Juan Aragon, Red Mike Malone and Reno Sloan. I stared 'em all in the eye and sent them over the mountains without a lick of fear. But Fargo? Before I met him, the only thing that ever shriveled up my dick was cold weather. Staring into his eyes made my pecker curl up like a bacon rind on a hot stove."

"Hell," Spider said in a nervous voice, "you ain't no lily liver, Russ. But you say he's twigged our game—think we should just maybe butt out now?"

"Nix on that. I ain't telling you all this to put snow in your boots. I'm telling you Fargo *ain't* just no nickel-novel hero. That means we got to do just like Spider's old pap use to say: Measure it twice, then cut it once. Any play we make has got to be smart and we gotta cover our ampersands—we make sure that if we don't kill him the first time out, we stay alive to kill him the next time."

Cleo frowned, not following all this. "That's too far north for me, Russ."

"Cleo, the end of your nose is too far north for you. Me and Spider will handle the mentality part of it—you just be ready to follow orders."

"What about the passengers?" Spider asked. "Did you figure out which one is on Lomax's payroll?"

"'Sides the actress—and, boys, she's a humdinger—there's a big-titted blonde I wouldn't mind drilling into. Way she looks at Fargo, he's prob'ly humping her already. But the three men—one's a bandy-legged preacher and one's a little butterball who flutters around like a nervous woman. But this third jasper, all togged out in a fancy white suit and a concho belt . . . he's one of them old boys who looks like he went to college but could lop your nuts off quick. I'd wager he's the one."

"You can't know with Lomax," Spider said. "He's tricky as a redheaded woman, and he just might find somebody Fargo wouldn't suspicion."

Alcott mulled that and nodded. His pale eyes followed the progress of the coach. "He just might, at that. We got to plant Fargo before he does, that's the main mile. I been thinking on that. And I think I got a plan."

Alcott pointed his chin toward the stagecoach. "I know that route good. The stage will roll until about ten tonight, then they'll lay over until sunrise at Hatch. Tomorrow night they'll rest at Caballo Lake. But if we kill Fargo at either place, that stage just might reverse its dust to El Paso. But two nights from now they'll lay over at San Marcial. That's too far north and no matter what happens, it makes more sense to just push on to Santa Fe. Lomax will shit a brick if it don't."

"All right," Spider said. "But I know that area around San Marcial. It *ain't* good ambush country—damn little cover. Cleo here is some pumpkins with his Sharps, but—"

"I got other plans for Fargo." Alcott cut him off. "Won't nobody need to draw a bead on Fargo. The station at San Marcial is run by Raul Jimenez and his sister. They put women passengers up in a little lean-to off the back of the house."

"Who gives a damn where the women sleep?" Cleo demanded.

"We do, knot head. See, they make male passengers sleep

on shakedowns Jimenez puts in the hallway right next to the front door—the opposite end from the women. That's real providential 'cause we don't want to kill the actress when we blow Skye Fargo to hellangone."

"Just how we gonna do that?" Spider asked.

Alcott's cruelly handsome face eased into a smile. He lit down from his roan and unbuckled the straps of a big pannier. He pulled out a small, sturdy cask.

"Boys, this here is blasting powder. That's thirty seconds of fuse poking out from the top. Enough powder to blow out a ton of solid rock. Lomax got it from one of his mining buddies. Two nights from now we're gonna sneak it up to the door of the San Marcial station and touch it off."

The other two men looked at each other and grinned. Then Spider looked at Alcott again. "That should do it, but are you sure it won't kill the actress?"

"Not if we set it back from the door at least fifteen feet. That should blow out the front of the station but leave the back standing—it's a good-size house and built solid."

"Yeah, but don't that mean we'll kill Lomax's mystery man?"

Alcott smiled as he tucked the cask away again. "If we're lucky. It'll kill all the men 'cept for Raul, and he's a gutless wonder we ain't gotta worry about. And then—who needs the motherlovin' stagecoach? Lomax just wants that bitch in his hands by June nineteenth, right? So we snatch her and take her north ourselves to Blood Mesa."

"Oh, *hell* yeah," Spider enthused. "We don't even gotta tell Lomax exactly when we get her there—we should have her all to ourself for at least a couple days."

By now Cleo was thoroughly confused. "Why would we want an actress?"

Spider and Alcott exchanged a mirthful glance.

"Don't worry, Cleo," Alcott assured him. "You'll figure it out."

By June twelfth, the third day of the stagecoach journey to Santa Fe, Fargo suffered a combination of sheer boredom and nerve-racking expectation. His hair-trigger alertness never wavered, a fact that tickled Booger no end.

"Look out, Fargo!" he shouted toward the end of the morning. "Oh, Jesus, Joseph and Mary! There's a big turtle up on the right. Could be an assassin."

"Just cut the capers and keep a weather eye out. That gunthrower back at Vado was no turtle."

"Ahh, you quivering old crone, that was two days ago. Did he show at Hatch or Caballo Lake? Just a drifter headed down to Old Mex. Son, you're building pimples into peaks."

"The fandango's coming," Fargo assured him. He removed his hat and whipped the dust from it. "Christ, not even noon and it's hot enough to peel the hide off a Gila monster."

"It'll be hotter when we meet in hell," Booger opined. He pulled his flask out of his shirt. "Kickapoo Jubilee will perk you up. Let's dip our beaks."

Fargo downed a jolt of the powerful Taos Lightning and shuddered as it mule-kicked him. He hadn't had a beer since his arrival in El Paso. And he missed his saddle after long hours on a hard seat.

Booger eyed the flask thoughtfully before he tucked it away. He lowered his voice conspiratorially. "Catfish, I'm horny as a brass band. When we bed down at San Marcial tonight, let's get them two dolly birds snockered and see can we play hide-the-sausage with 'em."

"Some knight of the ribbons you are. With me it's always the lady's choice."

Booger snapped the reins and splashed an amber streamer off the rump of the nearside wheeler. "Pah! Easy for you to say. You never get woman hungry like the rest of us poor, ugly bastards. They flock to you like flies to syrup. But I'm fearful, Skye, truly fearful. A man can explode into a thousand little pieces if he don't relieve the pressure."

Fargo shook his head in disbelieving wonder. "Booger, you're so full of shit your feet are sliding. You can't explode from being horny."

"Why, you soft-brain! It's been proved by them professors at them colleges in France and England. Proved by them as knows! See, a man is just like a volcano. He's got to have him a woman now and agin; got to relieve the pressure

38

inside him, or else he'll explode like a steam boiler. Look it up in the almanac."

"If you ever explode, you big galoot, you'll exterminate the buffalo. Well, you've always got Rosy Palm and her four daughters."

"True, thank God. The poor man's harem. It comforts a man to know he can hold his own."

Fargo used his army binoculars to scan the terrain all around them, cultivated fields to his left, arid flats and distant mountains on his right. All looked peaceful nor could he spot any good ambush points. Nonetheless, his inward eye kept seeing that two-gun trouble-seeker back at Vado with the shifty, bone-button eyes. Fargo's instincts told him an attack was soon coming and that he must be ready for it.

The readiness was all . . .

They reached the swing station at Lago Seco, and while the stock-tender switched out the teams the weary passengers climbed out to stretch out the kinks. Fargo handed Kathleen Barton out, astonished again at the woman's beauty. She wore her hair tucked up under a wide-brimmed straw hat with gay "follow-me-boys" ribbons streaming behind it in the hot breeze.

She surprised him by meeting his gaze frankly. "I place most men into three categories, Mr. Fargo: heroes, villains or fools. Our driver definitely fits that last category. But I'm not certain yet about you."

Fargo was about to reply to that unexpected comment when he was interrupted by Malachi Feldman. "Mr. Fargo, may I inquire as to which sign you were born under? I'd dearly love to work up your chart—for a nominal fee, of course."

Booger leaped down and almost squashed the little man. "Emigrate, you half-faced goat!" He brandished a fist as solid as a cedar mallet. "Or would you like a taste of the knuckle dusting?"

"Come down off your hind legs, Booger," Fargo snapped. "The doctor is harmless."

"Pah! He's a load in my pants."

Malachi backed discreetly away but stared spitefully at

Booger. "You, sir, have stars lined up in the Eighth House of the Zodiac. Your days are numbered."

The preacher had climbed out behind Lansford Ashton. He, too, glowered at Booger. "Repent, Mr. McTeague, before it is too late. Do not wait until you are on your deathbed, for there is no sudden leap from Delilah's lap to Abraham's bosom. You are bound for a fiery hell!"

"Turn off the tap, you spineless psalm singer. I will not leap from Delilah's lap until I've had full use of it. *You* may have Abraham's bosom to yourself, for you strike me as a sniveling sodomite. As for your fiery hell, I druther play checkers with Satan than a harp in heaven, for a man should be with his kin."

"I'm curious, friend," Ashton addressed Booger. "It strikes me as unusual that a man of your evident size and strength—and I might add rough-hewn intelligence—should bullyrag everyone around him, even women."

"Bullyrag, is it?" Booger narrowed his eyes. "Aye, you're a sly one. Spouting Latin and dressed like a peacock, yet I've glommed that pepperbox pistol in your valise. You've had it factory-rigged to fire all the barrels as one. How poor can a man's aim be that he needs to fire six bullets at once to hit his man?"

"A man who pauses to aim a handgun is likely to die, isn't that right, Fargo?"

"That's how I see it," Fargo answered calmly, holding Ashton's eyes until the man walked off to join the actress.

"Bad medicine," Booger muttered, watching him.

"I don't like him," Trixie said. "He looks like a gentleman, but he leaves a smear like a snail."

"A gentleman," Booger scoffed, "is a fool who gets out of the bathtub to piss."

"Did you really spot a pepperbox in his valise?" Fargo asked Booger.

"Did I speak Chinee, Trailsman? Aye, it was a pepperbox—with six beans loaded."

"Interesting," Fargo said.

As darkness settled over the Rio Grande Valley like a black cloak, Fargo lighted the coach's four oil-burning lamps, equipped with reflectors, for night driving. Almost three hours later they reached the station at San Marcial, their final destination until morning.

Fargo untied the Ovaro and the two team replacements and watered them before turning them out into the large paddock. All three horses were holding up well with the slow pace and lack of any weight to pull or carry. But the Ovaro, eager for a run, repeatedly bumped his nose into Fargo's shoulder.

"I know, old campaigner," Fargo soothed him, giving his withers a good scratch. "You ain't cut out for plodding along and neither am I. But we'll stretch out your legs soon."

Before he joined the others inside, Fargo grabbed his Henry and made a quiet search around the station in the buttery moonlight. He found no sign of human tracks or intruders, and the singsong cadence of insects suggested no one lurked nearby. Still, that uneasy prickle on the back of his neck had returned—the "truth goose" that often warned him of danger.

The surrounding, shape-shifting shadows hid trouble, and Fargo felt sure it would hit before sunrise.

He washed up at the pump out back, stood quietly listening to the night for a few minutes, then went inside.

This station, run by Raul Jimenez and his younger sister, Socorro, was one of the best on the line. The moment he stepped inside he saw the straw shakedowns in the short entrance hall, provided for male passengers. One of the men had lugged in a trunk for the actress and Fargo veered around it into the large main room.

The usual long trestle table dominated the room, but ladder-back chairs, scarred from spurs, replaced the benches. A big, doorless archway led into the kitchen, and Fargo spotted a roasting range of mud brick and mortar with a tin canopy over it to channel smoke and smells into a flue in the chimney.

Just then, Socorro Jimenez turned from the range to bring in a platter of biscuits and spotted Fargo. The pretty, shapely Mexican gave Fargo a welcome-big-boy smile as big as Texas—a smile he suddenly felt throbbing in his hip pocket. She wore a peasant blouse, baring one light brown shoulder,

41

and a wild cascade of dark hair framed her face with wanton appeal.

Well, now, Fargo thought, instantly recognizing the message those smoldering black eyes sent to him.

All the passengers except Kathleen Barton were already seated at the table.

"Mr. Jimenez," she said in her imperious tone, "will you kindly show me to the ladies quarters? I'd like to freshen up before evening repast."

"Pues, claro, senorita,*"* Raul replied, hovering around the great lady like a paid toady. "This way, *por favor."*

She gazed at the Trailsman. "If you're done ogling that serving girl, Mr. Fargo, would you kindly bring my trunk?"

Booger grinned wickedly. "He'll need a moment before he can walk right, muffin."

She stoically ignored this crudity, following Raul to the rear of the house. Fargo hoisted the trunk onto his back and trailed them.

"What is the meaning of *this?*" he heard her exclaim as he reached the slope-off room.

The Jimenezes had provided female passengers a small bedroom with a threadbare, rose-pattern carpet and a washstand with enameled pitcher and bowl.

"Pues, senorita, it is the best we can afford," Raul apologized.

"I don't mean the room. I mean *that.*"

She pointed to one of the iron bedsteads, its legs set in bowls of coal oil.

"That keeps the bedbugs off, Princess," Fargo informed her, struggling to keep a straight face. "Won't help much with the snakes, though."

"The . . . ?" Her face suddenly drained of color. Like an Indian at a treaty ceremony, Fargo had perfected the silent "abdomen laugh." By now, however, his belly ached.

"If one crawls in your bed during the night," he advised her, "don't move a muscle. I'll get it out in the morning. However, it may require some *groping* under the blankets."

"Oh, you'd love that!"

Fargo winked at her. "You'd love it even more. I'm . . . experienced in these matters."

She was on the verge of throwing the pitcher at him, so Fargo beat a hasty retreat. By now Socorro had laid the table with a veritable feast in Fargo's eyes: hot beef, chili beans and sourdough biscuits and tortillas. Booger had devoured a biscuit in one bite before Pastor Brandenburg spoke up.

"Sir! We have not said grace."

Booger quickly did the honors for him: "We thank the Father, the Son, and the Holy Ghost—he who eats the fastest gets the most."

Fargo tied into his meal with gusto, glancing up as Socorro returned to the kitchen for more biscuits. She shot him an inviting, cross-shoulder glance, the moist tip of her tongue quickly brushing her upper lip. Booger winked at Fargo. The human bear had already drained a half bottle of pulque, and Fargo sensed a hullabaloo coming.

The actress returned, clearly in a foul mood. She stared at the table as if it were piled with raw tripes.

"It ain't Delmonico's," Booger boomed out with his mouth full, leering at her. "But a hungry dog must eat dirty pudding. These beans're delicious."

"Beans?" Kathleen repeated in a horrified tone. *"Again?"*

"'S'matter, cottontail," Booger teased around his mouthful of food. "'Fraid you'll toot in front of us?"

She turned scarlet, which only egged the drunk reinsman on. Banging both fists on the table to keep the beat he bellowed out:

Beans! Beans! Good for your heart!
The more you eat, the more you fart!
The more you fart, the better you feel!
So eat your beans at every meal!

Like a professor proving a theorem, he suddenly tilted sideways on his chair, lifted one stout leg, and broke wind with resounding force.

"Did an angel speak?" he said innocently, staring at the petrified actress. Her face crumpled in disgust and revulsion and, as if spring-loaded, she stormed off in high dudgeon.

"Fox smells his own hole first!" he shouted to her retreating back.

Nonchalantly he reached across the table for her untouched plate.

"Ain't *she* silky-satin?" he barbed, scraping her supper onto his plate.

"Sir, you are a barbarian," the preacher announced.

"Sheep dip, Bible thumper. I ain't never shaved a man in my life. 'Course, I *have* cut a few throats in my day," he added with a menacing glower. "Ask Fargo."

Fargo, however, was staring into the kitchen, where Socorro was hidden from everyone's view but his. One hand reached up to tug down her peasant blouse, baring two beautiful tits that suddenly gave him an appetite for something besides good cooking.

"Think I'll have a look outside," he told the others, and Socorro smiled.

6

His Henry to hand, Fargo slipped out into the moonlit yard. Socorro's bold advances inside had lust throbbing in his blood, but even the rut need could not quell his gut conviction that serious trouble was about to erupt.

He circled the station, senses alert, Henry at the ready. For some reason he recalled his meeting in El Paso with Ambrose Jenkins and Addison Steele. Jenkins had quoted an anonymous letter sent to Kathleen: *Behold! The day cometh.*

The day being promised, Jenkins surmised, was the nineteenth of this month—the one-year anniversary of Kathleen's public and scornful rejection of Zack Lomax's marriage proposal. If Jenkins was right, her day was coming in one week.

But for Lomax to succeed, Fargo's day had to come sooner. The stagecoach was deep into New Mexico Territory now. Maybe Fargo's day was tonight. Maybe—

A foot scraped in the sand behind him and Fargo whirled, jacking a round into the Henry's chamber.

"Do not shoot me," a soft, heavily accented female voice called from the darkness. "There is something much nicer we both want, *verdad*?"

Socorro stopped in front of him, her eyes sheening in the moonlight. "I am shameless, I know. But I have no man, and always the fire burns inside me. Life here, Fargo—it is, how you say, boring. Men like you come to me only in dreams. The priest, he says that good girls always sleep with their hands outside the blankets. But I am bad—I dream of men like you and touch myself down below. Tonight I want to feel a real man inside me."

"You're going to, girl," Fargo promised. "Feel what your talk has done to me."

He guided her slim hand to the hard furrow along his left thigh.

"*Cristo!* Like a rock it is, and so big. Now *you* feel."

She guided his free hand under her blouse. Fargo was astounded—her breasts felt soft and hard at the same time, like trim muscles wrapped in smooth French wool. Instantly her nipples stiffened, poking hard into his palm. She moaned at his touch and began stroking the hard furrow until both of them were panting like overheated dogs.

Fargo grounded his Henry and opened his fly, freeing his straining, hungry manhood. He dropped his gun belt while she hitched her skirt high. Fargo knelt, gripped her hourglass hips, and pulled her down onto his lap. She gasped with eager pleasure as his curved saber parted the slick, pliant walls of her love nest.

"Hard and fast, Fargo!" she urged him. "Raul will soon miss me—oh! Yes, like *that*!"

Holding her firm ass tight, Fargo bucked hard, deep and fast, enjoying the mazy waltz after a dry spell of several weeks. Neither one showed the other mercy, driving each other to a frenzy of lust.

"Fargo, it goes so deep!" she panted in a hoarse whisper. "So deep, so *deep*!"

The angle was perfect for maximum stimulation of her magic button, and soon she was so galvanized with pleasure that each breath ended on a groan. Fargo felt the pinprickling in his groin swell to a massive, explosive release just as she climaxed in a series of hard, uncontrollable shudders.

The two of them, weak and dazed, collapsed sideways to the ground while their ragged breathing slowly returned to normal. After uncounted moments Raul's voice called out: *"Socorro! Donde estas?"*

With an effort she found her voice. *"Ya vengo, hermano!"*

"He knows why I came outside," she told Fargo as they untangled from each other. "And he will not be angry. But he does not want the others to know. Thank you, Fargo. I will always remember the stallion who took me under the stars.

And it will be very much time before my hands are again outside the blankets."

"Thank you, too, lady. This night's been a reg'lar tonic for me."

She kissed his lips and hurried toward the station. Fargo rose to his knees again, closed his fly, and buckled on his shell belt. A moment later he flinched hard when a voice bellowed from the house: "Ha-ho, ha-ho! Fargo, you double-poxed hound! You'll smell like fish all night!"

Fargo debated sleeping outside. But Booger slept like a dead man, and Fargo's deepening suspicion of Lansford Ashton made him reluctant to leave the house—he was, after all, Kathleen Barton's bodyguard. So he compromised by sleeping right next to the raw plank door.

Despite his torrid session out back with Socorro, sleep eluded Fargo long past the time the other three men nodded out—Booger snoring like a leaky bellows. He listened to the night sounds outside the door: the gentle soughing of the wind in the valley, the mournful howl of prowling coyotes, the monotonous rise and fall of insects. All of it eventually reassured him and gradually he floated down a deep tunnel into sleep.

Dream images danced across his sleeping mind, half formed, jumbled: Kathleen Barton's beautiful face, transforming into a mask of terror; pale-ice eyes promising hard death; a silver concho belt turning and twisting like a writhing snake and growing bloody fangs; a Concord swift wagon hurtling out of control into a black maw of hellish death.

And dream sounds, echoing a warning: the whinny of an agitated horse, then the almost comforting sound like meat sizzling in hot grease.

Meat sizzling louder and louder (*this is no dream, Fargo!*), but not meat, something else, something deadly, something he knew all too well (*the readiness is all, Fargo!*) . . .

Fargo's eyes blinked open and some inner urgency, the vital force to live, chased the cobwebs of sleep from his mind. Now he heard the Ovaro, nickering insistently to warn him, and realized: the insect noise was gone.

And that "meat sizzling"—there was a half-inch gap

under the door, and Fargo saw faint, flickering orange flashes of light, and he felt the cold sweat of dread break out in his armpits when he realized exactly how Death had come calling for him.

For a frozen moment his muscles seemed severed from his will, but it passed in a blink as a frontiersman's well-honed instinct to survive took over. Fargo catapulted to his feet, clawed at the latchstring, flung open the plank door. Clouds had mottled the bright yellow moon, and he squinted to see better in the stingy light.

There! Perhaps fifteen feet in front of the doorway—a dark shape spitting sparks!

Expecting his next breath to be his last, Fargo bound forward in several long strides. He could not risk trying to snuff the fuse, and instinct warned him the object was too heavy to kick safely away from the house.

Leaning far forward while still on the run, he scooped it up in both hands—a keg of blasting powder, he realized—and took three more giant strides while he brought it to his chest, then heaved with all the considerable strength of his arms, chest and shoulders.

As soon as he released it, Fargo dropped to the ground face-first like a dead weight. Even before he landed, hell turned itself inside out.

A crack-boom like the last ding-dong of doom threatened to shatter his eardrums. A blinding flash of white light was followed by a searing wall of heat. A giant, violent, invisible hand flung him back toward the house, which he slammed into before slumping to the ground.

The last thing Fargo was aware of was dirt and grass and stones slapping down hard all around him and a woman's bansheelike scream of terror from inside the station.

And his last thought: *the Great Thing at last.* . . .

"Is he dead?" Trixie said anxiously.

"I think he is breathing," Socorro said, holding a lantern over the unconscious Trailsman.

"He has a terrible bruise swelling on his forehead," Kathleen chimed in.

"Perhaps this will help him," Raul suggested, splashing a pail of water on Fargo's face.

"I fear he has departed this world," the preacher said. "May his soul—"

"One world at a time, witch doctor!" Booger snapped. "A conk on the *cabeza* will not kill Skye goldang Fargo. Don't get your bowels in an uproar, ladies—he'll come sassy."

The acrid stench of spent black powder hung heavy around the station house, and patches of wiry *palomilla* grass still snapped and sparked in the yard. Kathleen rushed into the house and returned with her silk reticule, extracting a small vial of sal volatile.

"Smelling salts should revive him," she said, uncapping the vial and passing it under his nostrils.

Fargo lay as inert as a stone slab.

"He *is* dead," Malachi Feldman asserted, his pudgy hands fluttering like nervous birds. "The Eighth House has claimed him."

"Pah!" Booger exclaimed. "You feckless ass. Only one thing can bring Fargo back from death's door: the scent of a woman's perfume. Give him your best toilet water, muffin."

Kathleen bristled like a feist. "*Stop* calling me muffin, you uncouth mudsill!"

"Beg pardon, cupcake. Give him a whiff of your finest aromatic—the stuff that gives men bedroom notions."

"Don't be ridiculous," she snapped, but she did extract a small bottle labeled Eau de Ciel and pull off the silver stopper. She held the bottle under his nose. "This couldn't possibly—"

A smile eased Fargo's lips apart as his eyes snapped open. For a moment he wondered if there was, after all, a heaven to which he had mistakenly been sent. Three pretty female faces hovered over his and—miracle to behold—Kathleen Barton's actually deigned to show some concern.

But this was not paradise—his head felt as if he'd been mule-kicked.

"Don't move yet," Ashton advised when Fargo groaned trying to sit up. "You may have a serious injury."

"Buncha damn mollycoddlers," Booger muttered. "Fargo, quitcher damn malingering."

He reached a brawny arm down and tugged Fargo roughly to his feet. "Come inside if you're feeling puny—a ration of who-shot-John will brace you."

Doctor Booger was right—a pony glass of whiskey did indeed perk up Fargo although his head still throbbed like a war drum. He sat at the trestle table, the rest crowding around him.

"Why, his eyebrows are singed!" Trixie said. "What happened out there, Skye?"

Fargo related what little he could about the powder cask.

"Perhaps a chunk of the wood did that to your head," Ashton surmised. "It was good work, Fargo. You saved the rest of us."

"No," Fargo corrected him, his eyes cutting to the actress. "I saved the men sleeping in the hallway at the front of the house. That powder charge was deliberately placed to spare anyone at the rear of the house—such as you, Miss Barton."

"I do not take your meaning, Mr. Fargo."

"Then I'll chew it a little finer—it was meant to kill me, your bodyguard, but keep you alive—until June nineteenth."

Fargo let silence underscore his point. Now she did take his meaning and the strength deserted her legs. She fell into one of the chairs.

Ashton watched her closely. "Notice how the lily chases the rose from the cheeks of our proud beauty."

She glanced at him sharply. "That's one of my lines from the romantic play *Fair Is the Rose*. I've noticed you are a cultured man, Mr. Ashton, but I wouldn't take you for an enthusiast of ladies' romances."

He bowed slightly. "Like the bee, I sample many flowers."

Interesting, Fargo thought. For a moment he recalled an image from his dream: a silver concho belt that turned into a snake with bloody fangs.

Kathleen aimed her bewitching eyes at the Trailsman again. "You mean, of course, Zack Lomax?"

"The very man, wouldn't you agree?"

After a few heartbeats she nodded. "My agent was right after all. And I dismissed that letter as hollow melodrama."

"We were both dunderheads, lass," Booger said in a rare admission of guilt. "I called long-shanks here a nervous old

50

woman for fretting constantly about danger. Now I see he is right, and this run will be no trip to Santa's lap."

"I understand your point about Fate," Kathleen said contritely. "Fate placed that powder keg outside the door—the cards you were dealt. But you 'played your hand' skillfully and saved many lives."

"Not Fate, Miss Barton," the preacher cut in, clutching his Bible in both hands and raising it for emphasis. "That is merely a roll of the dice. It is God's will that determines each man's destiny."

"Pious piffle," the astrological doctor protested. "Our destiny is determined by the alignment of stars and planets."

Booger brought one fist down on the table so hard that the whiskey bottle leaped two inches into the air. "Faugh! *Both* you chowderheads can chuck the gasworks and loop your buttons! It's almost sunrise and that swift wagon rolls with or without you weak sisters."

"But, Booger," Trixie protested. "Skye needs to rest. He—"

"He needs my boot up his hinder, is all. I promised to get him killed, and by the Lord Harry I will! He's damn lucky he wasn't bucked out while he was doing the deed outside with this hot little senyoreeter."

Socorro flushed and hurried out of the room. Raul threw his hands up toward the ceiling. *"Ay, dios!"* Booger watched Kathleen Barton stare at Fargo and grinned with pure malice.

"Well, that didn't take you long, did it?" she said snidely. "My noble bodyguard."

She returned to her room. Fargo stared at Booger. Abruptly, the two men burst out laughing like schoolboys.

"Scandalous," the horse-faced preacher said.

"If you say so, Rev," Ashton remarked. "As for me, I admire and envy Fargo for the conquest."

"Of course you do, slyboots," Booger said, narrowing his eyes. "You admire Fargo to death, eh?"

Trixie brought her lips close to Fargo's ear. When she whispered, her animal warm breath was a tickling caress.

"Skye? I sneaked outside and spied on you when you done that Mexican girl. Laws! My naughty parts been tingling ever since. The *size* on you—it took my breath clean away. I hope I'm next."

By the time the new team was hitched, the dark sky directly overhead was turning grainy with the promise of a new day. Only a few minutes later the newborn sun painted salmon-pink streaks over the eastern horizon. By the time the passengers were all aboard, the newly risen sun had begun to burn off the mist hovering over the nearby Rio Grande.

And now all could see the huge crater in the yard—as big as the Concord itself.

"This ain't the usual greasy-sack outfit we're up against," Fargo said grimly. "*These* boys are loaded for bear. And it's only June thirteenth."

Booger stared at the crater a few more moments and then cracked his blacksnake, the stagecoach jerking into motion with a rattle of tug chains.

"Bad medicine," he muttered to Fargo. "Powerful bad medicine."

Russ Alcott lowered his spyglass and cursed. "I ain't *even* believing this shit, boys! That motherlovin' station ain't been touched! And there's a big ol' hole way out in the yard."

"You sure you put the powder close enough to the house?" Spider asked. "I mean, it was dark and all."

"Does your mother know you're out? Christ, there was a full moon, and I paced off the distance from the door— fifteen feet. That crater is at least three times that distance from the house."

"Maybe it rolled," Cleo suggested.

Alcott aimed a withering stare at him. "Yeah, and maybe every Jack shall have his Jill, too. That ground is level as a billiard table. 'Sides, I dug a little wallow for it."

"Then Fargo got to it," Spider declared. "And the cockchafer musta done it just in the nick of time."

The three men were hidden behind a juniper brake near the river and had already watched the stagecoach leave.

"Lomax ain't gonna like this," Cleo fretted. "If Fargo ain't killed by—"

"It's too dead to skin now," Alcott cut him off. "The nearest mirror-relay man is up ahead at Bosque Grande. At ten o'clock sharp I'll send the signal that Fargo is still alive.

Lomax won't like it, but he knows damn good and well it'd be easier to tie down a bobcat with a piece of string than to kill Fargo. We still got plenty of time—losing a battle won't keep us from winning the war."

Alcott was quiet for several minutes, pondering options. Suddenly he made up his mind.

"Boys, that bosque just north of us is at least a ten-mile stretch of cottonwoods and pine that ain't been cleared for crops. Cleo, you may be a few bricks short of a load, but ain't nobody can shoot as plumb as you with a long gun. You're gonna get your chance to drop a bead on Fargo."

7

By late morning a glaring yellow sun was stuck high in the sky as if pegged there. Even the thoroughbraces couldn't spare Fargo's bruised head from constant jolts of pain when the Concord rattled over stretches of washboard trail or plunged into sudden dips.

"Booger, you spiteful son of a bitch," he complained at one point. "You're deliberately driving over the worst spots to deal me misery."

Booger loosed a guilty giggle like a boy caught playing with himself. "For a surety. If I cannot kill you all entire, it will be the death of a thousand ruts. *You* sneaked out last night for pussy, eh? And left old Booger to his blue balls."

Fargo shook his head in disgust. "What, I'm a pimp now? If you weren't so damn mean and ornery to women, you might get a little bit now and then. Cutting farts at the dinner table doesn't impress them."

"Pah! You hog it, Fargo! Next you'll prong Trixie—she's itching for you. But I guarandamntee, Fargo—you'll never play push-push with Her Nibs."

"That leaves me a broken man."

Booger jabbered on as if Fargo had not spoken. "No sir, Trailsman, you'll not point *her* heels to the sky. See, she's use to them yapping lapdogs in top hats and swallowtails. She needs to be took on the ground like an animal, is all."

"Get your mind off tail," Fargo snapped. "We got killers to waltz with. And a bosque coming up soon."

Again Booger ignored him, cracking his six-horse whip over the leaders in his irritation. "That high-toned bitch grates on a man's nerves, she does."

Fargo waved all this aside, pivoting around and climbing

onto the top of the coach. He gazed past the strapped-down trunks to check their backtrail. Roiling clouds of dust from the coach obscured the view, but with his field glasses he thought he could make out dust puffs far behind them.

He climbed back onto the box. By now Booger, who had never found any virtue in silence, had changed the subject. "*Look* at yourself, Fargo—you're poor as a hind-tit calf, just like me. Roving all over Robin Hood's barn, and for what? Mince pie, that's what! Why, a smart, handsome son of a bitch like you could've got hitched to a rich skirt and, as they say, managed her money for her."

"I begrudge no man who desires peace, safety and a comfortable life," Fargo replied. "But I've got jackrabbits in my socks, you know that. The moment I feel hemmed in, I push on. Besides, that monotonous, punkin-butter life holds no appeal for me. I'm a natural-born drifter and trouble seeker. And *this* stallion mounts the filly of his choice, not just one the law tethers him to."

"Spoke like a man, by God! You ain't as stupid as I look, catfish."

A few minutes later Fargo again climbed topside to inspect their backtrail. He shaded his eyes with his hand and closed them to slits against the glaring sun and swirling dust.

"Riders on our six," he called back to Booger.

"Red aboriginals?"

"Don't seem likely—they generally avoid the white man's roads and attack from the flanks."

"P'r'aps those hired assassins have give up on parlor tricks and decided to hug."

Again Fargo raised his field glasses and focused them finer. He spotted sombreros and crossed bandoliers.

"Mexican freebooters," he reported. "Maybe a dozen to fifteen, riding hell for leather and closing on us fast."

The lawless conditions in Mexico—where new "revolutions" were as frequent as the change of seasons—had given rise to closely knit bands of ruthless land pirates in the northern provinces of Sonora and Chihuahua. Disdainful of international boundaries, and leery of the Texas Rangers, they raided with impunity into New Mexico Territory knowing there was no organized authority to stop them. Fargo had faced their ilk before: kill-crazy marauders of no-church conscience who took a human life as casually as shooing off a fly.

"Hell's a-poppin'!" Booger roared gleefully. "Best way to cure a boil is to lance it. Now it's time for Booger's Law!"

Despite the danger pressing ever closer, Fargo couldn't resist a grin. He knew all about "Booger's Law" because surprise was one of Fargo's favorite tactics too: when being pursued, and unable to escape, sometimes the most effective action was to attack the attacker.

Booger reined sharply to the east, turning the team around on the dusty flat. Fargo grabbed the hoist rail and lowered the upper part of his body until his face was framed by one of the windows.

"We got a little barn dance coming," he warned the passengers. "Kneel down as low as you can and hang on tight as ticks—you're in for a wild ride."

Everyone obeyed except Kathleen Barton, who coolly ignored him and remained upright in her seat.

"You bolted down, Princess?" he demanded. "That order applies to everybody."

"I paid dearly for this seat, Mr. Fargo, and I have no intention of giving it up for that filthy floor."

"All right," Fargo said. "I'll send Booger down to enforce it."

She went pale as new gypsum and immediately crouched in the narrow space between her seat and the middle one.

"That's it," Fargo goaded just before he swung back up. "Say your prayers like a good girl."

"Beast!" she flung after him.

By now Booger had the swift wagon pointed due south and was whipping the six-horse team to a frenzy, his black-snake cracking and popping. "Hee-*yah*! Hee-*yah*, you spavined whores!"

Fargo braced his legs and climbed onto the roof of the wildly rocking coach. He went down flat between the trunks, laying the Henry's long barrel on the cargo rack to steady his aim. The freebooters, no doubt fortified by their numbers and Dutch courage, continued charging unabated.

The horsemen began chucking lead even before they

were within range. Fargo heard the insignificant popping sounds of their rifles, saw yellow geysers of sand begin to spit up from the ground out ahead. The Henry's long, rifled barrel gave it excellent accuracy, but Fargo was up against moving targets *from* a moving target, and he held his powder until the enemy's first rounds began snapping past his ears.

Even now Fargo would rather have waited longer, but one dead horse hanging up in the traces would halt the coach. He began levering and firing, laying his bead on riders and horses alike. Fargo hated like hell to kill horses, but given the number of riders and their brutal history he was intent only on reversing their dust.

Repeatedly the Henry bucked into his shoulder, brass casings glinting in the sun as they spat from the ejector port. Bullets chunked into the box and the top of the coach, but Fargo set his lips in grim determination and continued the lead bath.

A Mexican's face disappeared in a red smear and he was wiped from the saddle. A horse crashed to the ground, another, and now Fargo heard the solid reports of Booger's big-bore North & Savage—the gutsy driver had taken the reins in his teeth to free his hands. At first only one or two freebooters peeled off at the flanks and wheeled their mounts. But as the death coach hurtled ever closer, an unstoppable juggernaut of terror, the main body broke in a chaotic rout.

"Keep up the strut a little bit longer!" Fargo shouted down to Booger, fearing a false retreat—a favorite trick of Mexican raiders.

But the gang had supped full and didn't regroup for another charge. By now the team's bits were flecked with foam, and Booger reined them in to a walk to cool them out.

"Raggedy-assed greasers," he announced. "All gurgle and no guts. Hell, them snot-nosed cadets at Chapultepec put up more fight in the war of 'forty-seven. We best spell the team, Skye—they're blown in."

He pulled back on the reins and kicked the brake forward. Fargo swung down and threw open the doors. "Everybody all right?"

The women and Malachi Feldman were whey-faced with

fright. Lansford Ashton, however, seemed exhilarated. "We're fine, Fargo, thanks to you and that crazy-brave whip-master."

Pastor Brandenburg, clutching his big clasp Bible as usual, seemed oddly calm to Fargo. "You must be a veteran of shooting affrays, Preacher," Fargo remarked as he offered a hand to Trixie.

"Not at all, Brother Fargo. My heart is still in my throat. But we were all in the Lord's hands, and I had faith He would see us through."

"Sheep dip, witch doctor!" Booger scoffed, appearing beside Fargo. "It was two pagans with big *cojones* what saved your bony ass."

Fargo admired each woman as he handed them down. Kathleen looked quite fetching in side-lacing silk boots, a ruffled dress with pagoda sleeves, and a lace shawl. Her wing-shaped eyes were lined with just an alluring touch of kohl—a scintilla was currently fashionable among respectable ladies, but too much would be scandalous.

It was Trixie, however, who truly riveted both men's eyes. Her impressive breasts were on brazen display, pushed to spectacular height by stays laced tight as turnbuckles.

"Now here's something I don't quite savvy, Fargo," Booger said loudly enough for all to hear. "A woman will lay half of her jahoobies out to plain view as Trixie does. But will they show us an inch of the legs? Pah!"

"In polite society the word is 'limbs,'" the preacher corrected him as the three men began to pile out. "And proper ladies do not reveal that portion of their anatomies because they inspire concupiscence in men."

"Mebbe a dog will hump a leg," Booger said low in Fargo's ear, "but all *this* child yearns to see is fur and early morning dew."

"Bottle it," Fargo muttered, recalling Trixie's hot confession to him back at San Marcial station. "I'm horny enough just looking at Trixie—I don't need you stirring the coals."

In his irritation Booger forgot to keep his voice down. "Horny, is it—*you*? That's a banger! That little Mexer gal come in the house last night looking all-fired happy."

"She sure did," Trixie said, giving Fargo a tantalizing smile.

The actress goaded Fargo with a disdainful twist of her lips. "It seems your next conquest is at hand, Mr. Fargo."

Fargo touched his hat. "Hope is a waking dream, Miss Barton."

"Mr. Fargo, your sign *must* be the bull," the astrological doctor piped up.

"Oh, Fargo is full of the bull, right enough," Booger said, bulging a cheek out with his tongue.

Lansford Ashton laughed, enjoying all of it. "Miss Barton, some think I have a flair for composition. Perhaps there is enough material in this journey for a good play of the bawdy persuasion?"

"I am an actress, Mr. Lansford, not a temptress."

He bowed by way of apology. Fargo had the distinct impression that Kathleen had an unfavorable opinion of the man. This despite Addison Steele's assertion, back in El Paso, that the two of them would get along well. In fact, Fargo mused, nobody on this stagecoach seemed to like Ashton, nor did the man much care.

While the horses got a breather Fargo quickly ran a wiping patch down the Henry's bore and reloaded the tube magazine.

"Mr. McTeague," Kathleen said, "are we likely to reach a station soon?"

"Not until Los Pinos, Your Nibs, well after dark."

"Then I suggest we enjoy a nooning while the team rests. I have a few things I'll gladly share around. Mr. Fargo, will you kindly bring the wicker hamper on my seat?"

"Sure, let's get outside of some grub," Booger agreed eagerly.

The travelers moved to a small apron of shade under a pine tree beside the trail. Their eyes widened when she lifted the lid of the hamper: it was crammed with an astonishing array of delicacies, including pickled oysters, canned beef and ham, French rolls, cakes and confectionary of all sorts.

"No wonder you can spurn the way station food," Trixie said.

Fargo munched on a roll and a few oysters. While the rest finished their meal he checked on the Ovaro and the spare team behind the coach, feeding them a little crushed barley from his hat. The rig teams would soon be switched out at a swing station just before the stretch of cottonwoods and pines known as Bosque Grande.

As the passengers were reboarding, however, the actress made a little cry of distress, pointing at the top of the coach. "Oh! Look, one of my trunks is missing!"

"Strap must've broke during the hard run," Fargo said. "Don't worry—it'll be alongside the trail somewhere."

Fargo was right—they spotted it only a third of a mile north. But the trunk had opened on impact, scattering its intimate and feminine contents all over like confetti: slim chemises, velvet-trimmed cloaks, walking and carriage dresses, hats and ribbons and caps and bonnets, jackets, gloves and wrappers, a lace-trimmed corset cover—and Fargo's favorite, a pair of frilly red lace pantalets.

Booger whistled. "Christmas crackers! No wunner the horses been lugging since El Paso. And glom them dainties! Oh, Lulu girl!"

Fargo did glom them well as he helped the blushing actress gather up her belongings. He forced eye contact before surrendering the pantalets, which she quickly stuffed into the trunk.

"So you're an actress and not a temptress, huh?" he teased her. "Well, *that* was mighty tempting. Is that what you wear when you play Juliet?"

"Or the Whore of Babylon?" Booger taunted from up on the box.

"Oh, go to blazes you . . . you boorish, arrogant . . . oh, damn *both* of you rude bumpkins!"

She fled back into the coach and Fargo and Booger laughed so hard they almost dropped the trunk again.

8

Fargo's merriment, however, faded quickly as the coach rolled inevitably closer to the prime ambush region of the bosque.

"There's one more swing station before Los Pinos?" he asked Booger.

"Aye, but it's at Luna Bluff, Trailsman. And that means we hafta clear the hull damn Bosque Grande first—with a stale team that's already wore down to the nubs."

Fargo nodded, catching his drift. If trouble struck, they couldn't count on outrunning it.

"Addison Steele ordered me to stick with the coach at all times," Fargo said, thinking out loud. "But either we bend with the breeze or we break."

"Spell that out plain. I'm a simple son of a bitch and no boy for riddles."

"Lomax's hired guns need to kill me first. That blast last night at San Marcial was meant for me—they could easy have planted the charge at the back of the station if they just wanted to kill Kathleen. And that anonymous letter she got sounds to me like Lomax means to kill her himself on June nineteenth."

"Why, you glory-grabbing piker! They need to kill old Booger, too, happens they want to harm his passengers."

Fargo grinned. "Believe me, old son, I count on that. That's why I told your boss I would accept no driver but you. But see, it ain't likely that Lomax's dirt workers know that I've got a one-man army whipping this stage. To them, you're just a big bastard who blocks out the sun—an easy target they can't miss when they decide to shoot you. Assuming even a buffalo gun could drop you, which I doubt."

Fargo paused when the stage topped a low rise and he spotted the vast bosque, spread out like a dark painting before them, the Rio Grande looping through it. He had once contracted as a fast-messenger rider for the army in these parts and knew it was a bushwhacker's paradise.

"So let's *give* them me," Fargo resumed. "I'm gonna ride on ahead and let them have at it."

Booger mulled this, then nodded. "Needs must when the devil drives, eh? And the devil *is* driving this rig. Old Booger will make them dry-gulchers the sorriest sons of bitches in seventeen states if they come at this rig."

"I'll leave the double-ten," Fargo said, "so you'll have plenty of firepower. If I trusted that damn Ashton, I'd put him up here on the box with you—he looks like he could handle himself in a frolic."

Booger spat tobacco on the rump of the offside wheel horse. "Let's not and say we did. I'd sooner have a smallpox blanket wrapped around me. I'll wager a dollar to a dough-nut hole that oily-tongue sharper is on Lomax's payroll."

"I wonder," Fargo said, leaving it there. "See you in hell, pard."

He grabbed his Henry and tossed down his saddle and bridle. Then he swung off the box while the stage was still rolling at an easy pace. Fargo easily kept up as he untied the Ovaro.

"Where are you going?" Kathleen Barton challenged, poking her head outside.

"Crazy," Fargo called back. "Wanna come?"

"But you're supposed to be my bodyguard!"

"It's a body well worth guarding," he assured her as the coach rolled ahead of him.

She flushed with indignation and Fargo laughed, tossing her a two-finger salute.

"Say, chummies, this spot is perfect," Russ Alcott announced. "Damn fine cover and far enough off the stage road that we can make it to our horses if Cleo misses and Fargo comes after us."

The three outlaws had reached a tangled deadfall in the dense bosque. Gnarled cottonwoods, usually found only in isolated patches along western rivers, had grown in profusion along this stretch of the Rio Grande. Over the decades, America's heartiest tree—the pine—had filled in the open spaces between the cottonwoods' spreading branches.

"I ain't gonna miss," Cleo declared with the conviction of a love-struck groom saying "I do." He pointed east toward the narrow stage road. "Hell, that ain't but a hunnert yards or so, with a nice opening so's I can lay my bead. Old Patsy Plumb here"—he patted the hardwood stock of his carbine—"is gonna sink a big air shaft right through Fargo's skull."

The trio had left their horses hobbled along the river bank behind them.

"Even if Cleo misses," Spider Winslowe said, "Fargo ain't likely stupid enough to come at us, Russ, and just let us shoot him to rag tatters. Even afoot it's rough slogging to move through these trees. And he can't spot us anyhow."

"After the way that lanky fucker foxed us with the powder cask," Alcott said, "I ain't puttin' a *damn* thing past him. Don't get cocky, boys—this is a war, not a battle. I rate Fargo aces high as a survivor, and we ain't the first swinging dicks that figured to snuff his wick."

Spider thought about that and nodded. "You've packed heaven with plenty of fresh souls, Russ. If you rate Fargo that high, then I do, too."

"Smart man. Now you two wait here. I'm going out to the trail and watch for the coach. There ain't no way they can skirt the bosque, so they *will* be coming soon."

After swinging past the coach, barely ducking in time when Booger loosed a streamer at him, Fargo still had over a mile of open trail. The Ovaro was champing at the bit to stretch out the kinks, so Fargo gave the stallion his head and let him rip.

Fargo, too, welcomed the hard run and the familiar feel of a curved saddle under him. All too soon, however, the bosque loomed just before him, and Fargo was forced to rein his reluctant Ovaro back to a trot. A faster pace would put the Concord too far behind him and defeat his purpose of serving as a tempting target in place of the stagecoach.

The killers would be expecting him on the coach, and since the shotgun rode to the left of the driver, that meant any ambush would come from west of the trail. As Fargo entered the dense woods, immediately feeling relief from the broiling afternoon sun, he reined in for several minutes to let his eyes adjust to the dimmer lighting.

While he sat his saddle, waiting, he put his years of scouting experience to work. He sent his hearing out beyond the near distance, listening for the scolding of angry birds disturbed at human intrusion, or the warning calls of animals. Most of all, however, he kept close watch on the Ovaro's sensitive nostrils and ears—his most reliable sentries when hidden danger lurked nearby.

Fargo slid his Henry from its boot and jacked a round into the chamber, setting the gun's butt plate on his right thigh, muzzle pointing at the sky.

"All right, old warhorse," he said softly, squeezing the Ovaro with his knees, "once more into the breach."

Spider and Cleo watched their leader quickly wend his way back through the trees to their position.

"Fargo's coming," he announced. "But he's horsed."

"Shit," Spider said. "That means Cleo has *got* to score with his first shot. That stallion of his runs like his pa's name is Going and his ma's name is Fast. What's his pace?"

"Just a slow trot. He's deliberately making himself a target. That tells me he *don't* plan on skedaddling. Spider's right, Cleo—you *got* to pop Fargo over with your first shot."

"Why'n't we just kill his horse with the first shot?" Spider tossed in. "Bigger target."

"Nix on that. Fargo *will* come at us then, with blood in his eyes—you can take that to the bank. He wasn't born in the woods to be scairt by an owl. He don't sleep in rented rooms, boys—we're on *his* terrain now. Cleo, quit scratching your ass and snap in! He'll be showing in that little clearing in about two minutes. You'll have maybe ten seconds to get on bead and squeeze one off. Don't bollix it, boy."

Cleo dropped into a kneeling offhand position and swung the butt of his Sharps securely into his shoulder socket. Soon all three men heard it—the faint, muted thud of shod hooves moving slow over dirt.

Moments later Cleo spotted horse and rider. He drew his hammer from half cock to full with a faint, metallic click. He slipped his finger inside the trigger guard and inhaled a long breath. He expelled it slowly while he relaxed his muscles.

Squeeze, he reminded himself as he dropped the bead just under the brim of Fargo's white hat—only a head shot could guarantee a one-bullet kill.

Just squeeze . . . the slightest bucking of the trigger would throw off his aim.

His trigger finger took up the slack in one long, continuous pull.

Sweat beaded and trickled out from Fargo's hair, tickling his forehead. As he rode deeper into the bosque he could feel his enemy's eyes on him. It was useless, in this dense growth, to hope he could actually spot them. Nor could he even make a smart guess as to which stretch of the trail made for a good ambush spot. He felt like a bedbug on a clean sheet—easy to see and nowhere to hide.

The Ovaro, too, was nervous in this dim tunnel and constantly snuffed the ground. Fargo didn't pull his head up, knowing that smelling the ground settled a horse in unfamiliar surroundings.

Fargo had already sheathed his Henry. Only fifty yards into the trees he had realized the long-barreled gun would be useless here. He knew that—assuming he wasn't blasted out of the saddle—it would not be enough to simply toss some lead and hope the killers fled.

He had to make it hot for them—so hot they got scared and cleared out. That meant "Booger's Law" again—attack the attackers, and a long-barreled gun would only hinder him in these close-packed trees.

You never hear the shot that kills you.

Fargo willed himself calm and attentive, trying to hear above the pounding of his heart in his ears.

The readiness is all. . . .

The moment was coming, he sensed that, believed in it

the way a Baptist believed in Jesus. It would be brief, crucial to his existence—that one little clue that most men missed or couldn't read. A change in the insect hum, perhaps, or that sixth-sense sudden warning in the air, when it felt charged like it sometimes did before a massive crack of lightning.

Or when the Ovaro's ears suddenly pricked forward as they had just now.

Here was the fandango, and Fargo did not pause to think—with the instincts honed from long survival in a harsh land, he simply reacted from reflex, slumping hard to the right side only an eyeblink before a slug thwacked into the tree right beside him. Almost simultaneously he heard the precision crack of a rifle.

Fargo still held the reins and tugged the Ovaro into the cover of the trees as a withering hail of bullets chunked in around them. He quickly wrapped the reins around a weak branch—if he were killed, the Ovaro could easily break free and avoid the fate of becoming an outlaw horse, for no sane man would kill such a mount.

Fargo had six beans in the wheel of his Colt, six more in the spare cylinder in his possibles bag. Hooking left to get out of the line of fire, he sprinted across the trail, letting his experienced ears give him a good idea where the shooters were. Moving quickly and with instinctive dexterity, he leap-frogged from tree to tree, firing as he moved, run and gun.

The enemy fire abated and he heard a man shout, "Pull foot, boys!" Fargo homed in on that voice, pressing forward and changing cylinders as he moved. Firing a round every five seconds or so, he heard the frantic rustle of branches as his attackers panicked.

Even when his twelfth shot was fired Fargo didn't give up. He paused only long enough to thumb reloads into his Colt, then resumed his run-and-gun pursuit. He had to frazzle their nerves enough that they would lack the fighting fettle for another ambush attempt in the bosque.

Then, just before he reached the Rio Grande, he heard hooves pounding toward the north in the three-beat drumming of a gallop. They were escaping along the grassy bank of the river, and more foot pursuit was folly.

Fargo heaved a sigh and leaned against a cottonwood for

a moment, his legs trembling now that it was over—at least for now. The shootout and the pursuit were piddling and he had faced no grave danger. But the suspense leading up to that first shot, and the narrow miss, had taken its delayed toll on his nerves.

"Fargo," he muttered as he recruited his strength for the return to his horse, "maybe you *could* stand a little of that punkin-butter monotony."

The El Paso to Santa Fe stagecoach cleared Bosque Grande without further incident. The valley opened up again and Fargo breathed easier. By late afternoon they reached the swing station at Luna Bluff and acquired a fresh relay team.

"All them gunshots back in them trees," Trixie remarked to Fargo as the passengers stretched their legs at the swing station. "Didja kill anybody, Skye?"

"Pah!" Booger interceded, ogling her pulchritude. "The man admits he spent damn near eighteen cartridges and shot nothing but trees. Up in Dakota he once tried to take a scalp and it made him puke. And can he drink Indian burner like a man?"

The preacher overheard this. He stared at Booger, the corners of his mouth turning down in a frown. "Can any good thing come out of Nazareth?"

"Ahh, go blow your horn, Gabriel. I'll credit no man who claims a virgin can have a baby. And I s'pose oysters can walk up stairs?"

Pastor Brandenburg clutched his Bible like a drowning man clinging to a log. "Satan, get behind me!"

"Aye, you'd like that, eh? Buggered by Beelzebub. *That* would leave you slouching toward Bethlehem."

"Whack the cork," Fargo snapped. "He's a preacher and you're a blasphemer. How do you expect him to act?"

"Blasphemy, is it? Old Booger knows shit from apple butter," Booger groused as he walked away to help the swingman with the traces.

"Mr. Fargo," Kathleen said, "do you expect those men to attack again?"

"Sure as sun in the morning. I'd say Zack Lomax went to a mort of trouble to get vengeance on you."

"Is the man a Capricorn?" Malachi Feldman interceded. "A man born under the influence of Mars is bellicose, certainly. But even worse is a Capricorn. They—"

"Miss Barton has no interest in your inane prattle," Lansford Ashton cut in harshly. "Nor do the rest of us. I prefer an honest pickpocket to your ilk."

Kathleen ignored all of this, still watching Fargo. "It has occurred to me, Mr. Fargo, that you are facing great danger to protect me. I hope you realize I'm grateful."

Her tone implied that she was praising a servant for getting the carpet extra clean.

"I'm getting good wages for it," Fargo replied. "It's just a job."

He grinned when he saw scarlet points suddenly appear on her finely sculpted cheeks. She stiffened, then abruptly returned to the coach.

Interesting, Fargo thought.

The Concord swift wagon resumed its trek toward the station at Los Pinos. Booger tipped his flask now and then and belted out bawdy verses while Fargo kept a close eye on the surrounding valley. Booger suddenly burst out laughing, slapping his tree-trunk thigh.

"Oh, Skye, Her Nibs will likely have a catfit when we get to Los Pinos. You know the place?"

Fargo shook his head. "Why? What about it?"

But Booger only smiled mysteriously. "Why, you'll see. *I'm* not the boy to ruin a surprise."

"You're mighty rough on that gal. Why'n't you ease off a bit?"

"I, rough on the Quality? That's a libel on me, longshanks. Why, she's a reg'lar peach of a woman. I'm merely having a bit of sport with her."

Booger cracked his blacksnake over the leaders. "Gee up, you lazy animules! Get up! Hi yi! Fargo, straight arrow now: Do you b'lieve this Ashton yack works for Lomax?"

"I think he's shiftier than a creased buck, and I'd never leave my horse with him. I ain't so sure he's with Lomax, though. He can't be unless Lomax knew which coach Kathleen was taking."

"Fargo, is your brain any bigger than your pee hole? First

the bomb, then the attack today—ain't it obvious as a third tit that Lomax knows the very coach she's on?"

"*Now* he does, sure. But recall that gunslick at the Vado station—he coulda been there as a spotter. The real poser is—did Lomax know *before* the coach pulled out of El Paso? That's the only way he could plant a man on it."

Booger said, "Look here, catfish—Lomax is s'pose to be deader than a dried herring. What if it ain't him behind all this?"

"He's the only one that fits the known facts. There's no proof he's dead, either."

Fargo was silent for a minute, thinking. "Could your boss—Addison Steele—be bought?" he finally asked. "Paid off to tell Lomax what stage she was taking? It was in the newspapers that she was coming to Santa Fe from El Paso."

"Yes, he could be bought like most men, but not in any plan to kill a woman. And *this* woman? Addison owns stock in Overland—why, if anything happens to America's Sweetheart on an Overland run, it could sink the company. And Steele would be cashiered, for a surety."

Fargo nodded. "That rings right. But he's not the only one Lomax could bribe, is he?"

"Naw. Overland is packed up the wazoo with pus-guts and board walkers—assistant managers, clerks and such. The green eyeshades, I calls 'em. Why, I'd say it's an even bet Lomax knew in time to put a curly wolf on the passenger list. And Ashton—I like him for it."

"Mm. If so, it's not his job to kill the actress. Seems like Lomax wants that pleasure for himself. Most likely, it's Ashton's job to kill me if the others come a cropper."

"Happens that's so, why, he'll have to kill old Booger, too."

"Well, he's got a pepperbox in his valise—six bullets fired at one time would drop even an ox like you. Then he could just steal my horse and abduct Kathleen."

Booger looked over at him, his moon face set in a frown. "It could play out that way right enough. We best watch that bastard, Skye—watch him like two cats on a rat."

9

Three hours after Fargo lit the four night-running lamps, Booger reined in at Los Pinos.

The place was hardly more than a dilapidated shack caving in on itself. In the silver-white moonlight it reminded Fargo of deserted hovels he had seen in depleted mining camps. No smoke curled from the stovepipe chimney, and no light showed through the flyspecked, oiled paper serving as windows. An open-fronted stock shed stood empty and Booger had already informed him that Los Pinos could offer no fresh relay because of manpower shortages.

"This place looks abandoned," Fargo said as he prepared to swing off the box. "Maybe there's been trouble."

Booger was unable to stifle a giggle. "Oh, there *is* trouble, catfish, count on it," he said, volunteering no more.

Fargo swung the step into place and helped the weary ladies out. Kathleen Barton gaped in astonishment. "*This* is a station? Mr. McTeague, you gave me to understand there were bathing facilities here!"

"Why, yes, Your Nibs. There's a pump around back, and as you can plainly see, a water trough. When the horses have finished drink—"

"I shall protest this outrage!" she enunciated crisply. "I will have your job for this!"

By now Booger was shaking with mirth. "Why, cottontail, you may have it for the asking—I'll not deprive you."

Fargo stifled a laugh, lifting the latchstring and stepping inside. The place was as dark as the inside of a boot and filled with the stench of whiskey and boiled cabbage. Even fouler, however, was the stink of antiquated fish-oil lamps.

Somebody farther inside the room was snoring with enough racket to wake snakes.

Fargo found one of the old lamps hanging by the door. He snapped a phosphor to life with his thumbnail and fired up the wick. Dirty yellow light filled the room, pushing shadows back into the corners.

"My God!" Kathleen said in a shocked whisper, peering around Fargo.

The light annoyed a rat, which ambled back to its nest in a back corner filled with rubbish. Several empty whiskey bottles dotted the rammed-earth floor, and the only "furnishings" were empty nail kegs and a table made from a door nailed to a pair of sawhorses.

An old man who looked to be straight out of Genesis and sprung in the knees was fast asleep on a tatty buffalo robe. His face was as wrinkled as a whore's bedsheet, and a tobacco-stained beard covered most of his caved-in chest. He wore frayed canvas trousers—gone through at the knees—and a shirt sewn from old sacking.

"Roust out, Methuselah!" Fargo sang out.

The old codger woke with a violent start, shading his eyes from the light.

"Katy Christ, mister," he croaked, struggling to his feet with a loud cracking of stiff joints. "Scare the bejabbers out of a fellow, why'n'cha?"

"Don't tell me you're the station master?"

"Why not tell you, it's God's honest truth. My name's Pow—that's bobtail for Powhatan. 'Bout damn time you folks got here—I waited up long as I could."

Kathleen, Trixie, Malachi, Ashton and the preacher all stood crowded outside the door, perhaps daunted by the hellish stench. They stared with paralyzed stupefaction.

"Well, don't stand there gawking like chawbacons at a county fair," he admonished from a sullen deadpan. "C'mon inside—you're lettin' flies in."

"I'd wager they're trying to escape," Fargo remarked, casting his eye around the rubbish-strewn room. Booger was unhitching the team out in the yard, and Fargo heard him roaring with laughter.

"Shall I draw your bath now, Miss Barton?" he barely managed before more laughter choked him. Fargo laughed, too, and shook his head.

"Mr. Fargo, it's *not* humorous!" Kathleen shot at him, stamping her foot in frustration. "Perhaps you and—and 'Booger' are used to such abominable conditions, but I am not!"

"Hear, hear," the preacher said. "It's not fit for pigs much less ladies."

"*How* can Overland treat its passengers this way?" Kathleen demanded. "By contract we are promised hot food, clean accommodations, and the opportunity for at least one hot bath. And where are we to sleep—on this filthy floor?"

Pow got his first good size-up of the actress, squinting in the lamplight as if gnats were swarming his eyes. He loosed a whistle. "Pretty as four aces and brash as a rented mule. You'll have your eats, Little Miss Pink Cheeks."

He winked at Fargo. "Jest today I got in a fresh load of fat, sugar-cured Salt Lake grasshoppers. Them's good fixin's."

Methuselah picked up a quirt from the crude table and snapped it at a fly, squashing it dead. "Got two that time," he boasted. "Must be mating season."

"I will *not* eat grasshoppers," Kathleen flung at him.

He grinned at her, yellow nubbins of teeth visible through his beard. "Look who's feelin' a mite scratchy tonight. You two pretty gals may sleep on my buff robe."

"And catch fleas? I will pass on that wondrous opportunity. The stench in here is unbearable."

Pow winked at Fargo. "Oh, thissen's silk, all right. Pure silk."

"And when was the last time," Kathleen steamed on, "you laundered your clothing?"

"Well, I ain't got no Sunday-go-to-meetin' togs like concho belt there, Your Bitchiness."

Fargo was enjoying all this but now it was time to intercede. Kathleen had every right to be angry. But Fargo was dog tired and so was everyone else.

"Miss Barton," he said mildly, "why push if a thing won't move? You still have plenty of eats in your hamper. Far as

72

sleeping arrangements, I'm not bedding down inside this rat-trap, either. I suggest you and Trixie sleep in the coach, and the rest of us will bed down in the stock shed."

"You folks oughter keep a weather eye out while you head north," Pow warned. "They was an express rider through here today. Says 'Paches is raiding up that way. The station house at Polvadera was burnt down. They kilt the station master and his woman but spared the children. Sons-a-bitches also raided the swing station at Lemitar and killed the relays. It was that bunch under the renegade Red Sash."

This news doubly alarmed Fargo. Polvadera was the next scheduled station before La Joya, and with the swing station at Lemitar down, this team would be dangerously over-worked.

"Yeah, I've seen Red Sash's handwork," Fargo remarked. "His bunch left nine men dead at the silver mines of the Santa Rita over in Arizona."

Fargo knew they also raided with impunity in New Mexico knowing that, if pursued, they could flee south to the lava-bed country and the desolate alkali pan known as Jornada del Muerto, the Journey of Death. Fargo had barely survived it once, and no one was foolish enough to follow Apaches there.

"Apaches," Ashton said, his normally nonchalant tone now tense. "No boys to fool with. I was under the impression they were hiding down in the Dragoon Mountains and harassing Mexicans."

"To them," Fargo replied, "the entire New Mexico territory has been *Apacheria* for centuries. That bunch you're talking about is only the Coyotero branch of the tribe. Red Sash and his renegades are Jicarillas. They're raiders and they don't put down roots anywhere."

"God preserve us," the preacher said.

"Skye," Trixie said, "do Apaches . . . I mean, when they capture white women, do they . . . ?"

"They'll rape the living shit outta both you beauties," Pow interjected bluntly. "And then they'll either stone you into silence or take you along fir the bucks to enjoy every night when they git shellacked on tizwin—that's corn beer. But there's good news, too."

73

By now Kathleen had been stunned out of her indignation, which was replaced by tight-lipped fear. "Good news? You say we'll be outraged and murdered. How could there possibly be good news?"

Pow quirted another fly. "Apaches don't scalp, little lady. You won't have to lose that beautiful hair."

By midafternoon of June fourteenth, Zack Lomax was nervously pacing back and forth in his study, gesturing with both hands.

"Damn it, Olney, I'm starting to worry. It's a ten-day run from El Paso to Santa Fe, and they're now halfway here. You're certain this latest mirror relay was interpreted correctly?"

"'Fraid so, boss," Olney Lucas replied. "Congreve and the rest of the team know the signal system real good—I tested them all. Today's message from Alcott is that they failed to kill Fargo at Bosque Grande."

"Shit, piss and corruption! That's two failures now. The chances for any further attempts diminish greatly until well north of Albuquerque—it's mostly open and level country along the Overland route. I was hoping Russ's bunch would point Fargo's toes to the sky by now."

Olney cleared his throat. "Just calm down, Mr. Lomax, and remember what you always tell me—you planned this out for one full year. You anticipated trouble and you knew you'd need safeguards. There's still plenty of time, and the odds look mighty grim for Fargo."

"And now these goddamn gut-eating Apaches," Lomax stewed. "Jesus, talk about irony. One year of planning, thousands of dollars to execute those plans—all so that *I personally* can balance the ledger by killing the bitch with my own hands. And here a bunch of half-naked red savages might beat me to it."

"Yeah, but at least she'd be dead."

Olney realized the remark was unwise when his employer's burning, preternatural eyes drilled into him, piercing like bullets. "You pathetic idiot! We'll *all* die eventually, won't we? The question is how and who's in control of it. The point is to make her realize, in her last terrified seconds, that

I am the master of her fate—that her signature on that vicious letter to the newspaper one year ago also signed her own death warrant."

This time Olney wisely held his tongue. Watching Lomax now, the hard angles and planes of his face a mask of soul-searing rage, those intense eyes were windows on a mind rotted by insanity and the lust for revenge. All this because a piece of uppity quiff gave him the mitten—you had to handle a man like that the same way you'd handle unstable nitro.

"Fargo," Lomax said suddenly, abruptly picking up the thread he'd dropped. "It's irony heaped *on top* of irony. All of a sudden I have to hope Fargo *does* stay alive long enough to stave off this Apache threat."

"Yeah, but don't forget your safeguard," Olney reminded him. "Fargo can't know you got a man on the coach. Hell, you kept that so secret even I don't know who it is. If Russ and the boys botch it, he can kill Fargo."

This reminder, however, evoked a worried frown from Lomax.

"You forget something, Olney. Remember Alcott's report that the stagecoach driver has not been relieved for hundreds of miles? Haven't you figured that one out by now? Whoever that driver is, Fargo handpicked him. If he trusts the man that much, count upon it—he is both trustworthy *and* capable."

"I take your drift. He has to get the drop on both of them. Still—if they don't suspect one of the passengers, it can't be that hard to just back-shoot the two of them. Since you picked this man yourself, you must have confidence in him."

Olney's remark heartened Lomax for a moment. Everything in his face smiled except those strangely luminous, insane eyes. "You've put the axe on the helve. He's the best money can buy."

Abruptly, however, the smile faded from his face like a snowflake melting on a river. His features turned hard as granite.

"But I *don't* want to use him to kill Fargo, don't you see? Because then his cover is exposed and he has to kill the driver, too. That throws all my plans into disarray. That would force him to abduct her and get her to Santa Fe, and given who she is, that triggers a manhunt."

"It would at that," Olney agreed. "We're talking America's Sweetheart here."

"It's the damn *timing*, Olney, don't you see it? This man's job is to strike at Blood Mesa on the nineteenth, with Fargo already out of the picture. He kills the driver and the passengers when it's far too late for any authorities to intervene."

Lomax crossed to his desk and picked up the Spanish dagger he had purchased just for one occasion, gazing fondly at it as if it were a beloved child.

"When you thrust steel deep into vitals, Olney, and give it what's called the Spanish twist, you can actually feel the victim's body heat rush out on to your hand. I won't, I *can't*, let Fargo ruin this for me! One way or the other he must be killed before Blood Mesa."

By late afternoon the exhausted team could not be whipped past a walk.

"Pah!" Booger slipped his six-horse whip into its socket and cursed in disgust. "Bad medicine, Skye. We'll hafta rest and water 'em soon or we'll all be riding shank's mare."

Fargo nodded, his eyes narrowed to slits as he minutely studied the surrounding landscape. The vast western sky stretched to infinity all around them, only a few ragged tatters of cloud in a dome of china blue. Distant mountains—the Manzano Range—saw-toothed the northeast horizon, but the agriculture had thinned out toward the Rio Grande just west of them. The terrain around them now was mostly yellow-brown and arid, dotted with creosote bushes and greasewood.

"Them hawk eyes of yours spotted any sign of Apaches?" Booger demanded.

Fargo shook his head. "But that's what troubles me," he admitted. "It's bad enough when you see Apaches, but at least you know where they are. It's worse when you don't see them."

"Skye?"

Fargo leaned sideways and looked over his shoulder. Trixie's anxious face hung out the window. "What, m'heart?"

"Back yonder at that burned-out station, Pol—Polva—"

"Polvadera."

"Yes. I seen you hunkered down on your heels studying the ground for a long time. What didja figure out?"

"Well, judging from the prints—especially the overlaps—I'd guess we got about twenty renegades raiding in these parts. Their mounts are a mix of shod horses, likely stolen from whites, and unshod mustangs stolen in raids on other tribes. After the raid they headed due east."

"Twenty," she repeated, biting her lower lip. "Are they gonna attack us?"

"How long is a piece of string? All Indians are notional. Could be they left these parts for better targets."

"Twenty," she said again, and Fargo saw her chin tremble. Still thinking, he realized, about what Methuselah told them last night at Los Pinos, the stupid old goat.

"Listen," he told her firmly, knowing that Kathleen, too, was hanging on every word, "there's no call to go puny. Everybody back in the land of steady habits believes all wild Indians are expert horsemen. But Apaches are mostly indifferent to horses—most would as soon eat one as ride it. They prefer sneak attacks on foot, but the open country around here forces them to ride."

"That's good?"

"Hell yes, it is. We'd be in a lot tighter spot if this was twenty Comanches or Kiowas. They practically live on their horses. But with Apaches, a mounted attack won't be near as dangerous."

"You mean, you think we got a chance?"

His sturdy white teeth flashed in a smile. "Honey, I *always* plan to win."

The wink he gave her told her his boast included winning with women, and she encouraged his confidence with a flirtatious smile.

Malachi Feldman poked his head outside. "What about the others, Mr. Fargo? The white men who attacked you yesterday—think you scared 'em off?"

"They're mercenaries," Fargo replied, "and not likely to draw most of their wages until they finish the job. But they ain't stupid enough to try attacking us in this open country. They'll send in their card later, but I'd wager we're all right for now."

Fargo said nothing about the mirror flashes he and Booger had spotted earlier today. Flashes traveling in relay—and both men knew there were no U.S. Army mirror stations along this route.

"'Honey, I *always* plan to win,'" Booger mimicked when Fargo turned back around. "You'll play push-push with her next while old Booger will be forced to skin the cat. Well, you best poke her quick, catfish. What you told Trixie just now—that was turning dung into strawberries."

"How you figure that?"

"Happens them 'Paches notch their sights on us, it won't matter a jackstraw how piss-poor they ride. You know damn good and well them red sons is some pumpkins at marksmanship, and they got plenty of rifles. Most Injins count on big medicine to guide a bullet, but 'Paches have learned to aim. Twenty raiders agin two of us, Fargo."

"Ain't *you* the sunshine peddler. There's three other men along."

Booger howled like a dog in the hot moons. "*Men?* Fargo, this ain't no peyote dream. The God-monger and the stargazer is both worthless cheese dicks. Hell, neither one of 'em is even heeled."

"Ashton has got mettle in him. And his pepperbox will chuck plenty of lead in a close-in fight."

"Aye, but he's saving them whistlers for me and you." Booger loosed a streamer, barely missing Fargo. "Use to was, you found only by-God *men* west of Big Muddy. Now it's all these mail-order yacks wearin' pretty conchos and dressed in reach-me-downs from stores. Christmas Crackers! These gussied-up dudes like Ashton would starve and go naked without stores."

Booger was a complainer by nature, but Fargo knew he was right in the main. It had already begun: the methodical destruction of the American West, soon to be incinerated to ashes by the inflammatory gas of "expansionist" politicians and their sidekicks, the merchant capitalists and their new "investment consortiums." The buffalo, once found in thundering herds numbering into the hundreds of thousands, was now on the wane, and the Plains tribes would inevitably follow. And before too long, the one-man outfits like Skye Fargo,

78

too, would be relics of the past, ground up in a profiteering onslaught of mines, railroads, timbering and farming.

Booger's voice sliced into his ruminations. "Eyes right!"

Fargo glanced east and felt his stomach knot into a fist. Puffs of dark smoke were rising above the horizon.

"Apaches," Booger announced. "And that smoke talk is all about us."

10

By turns Booger cursed, nursed and cajoled his exhausted team northward, resting them a few minutes every half hour. Fargo helped him harness the two spare bays into the lead, but the stronger horses were fighting four weaker ones and the coach still plodded along slower than a man walking.

The afternoon had begun to fade as they reached the time of day Fargo called "between dog and wolf," neither day nor night.

"Fargo, this shit's for the birds," Booger announced. "Mayhap we can reach La Joya by midnight or thereabouts, but this stretch of the road is called the Kidney Crusher— filled with washouts and holes. We'd hafta use the running lights or risk busting an axle, if you catch my drift?"

Fargo caught it. Apaches were not constricted, as were many other tribes, by superstitious taboos against nighttime warfare. Like the fierce Comanches, they did some of their bloodiest work in surprise raids after dark. And those four bright running lamps would be beacons guiding them to the slaughter.

"I'll scout ahead and find us a spot to camp," Fargo said. "The team needs a long rest. And we'll be safer if we fort up. When you hear me fire one shot, bring the rig forward."

He tossed down his tack and climbed off the coach. Kathleen poked her head out. "Where are you going, Mr. Fargo? And please don't tell me 'crazy' this time."

He explained the situation to the others. "You folks might's well step out and stretch your leg—uhh, limbs," he corrected himself, grinning at the actress in the grainy twilight. "But stay close to the coach. Ashton, can you work a Henry?"

"I'm no marksman with a rifle, but I know how to work a repeater."

"I'll leave it with you." Even if the man was working for Lomax, Fargo reasoned, he wouldn't try anything now—he had no horse to escape on, and he needed Booger and Fargo in the face of this Apache threat.

Kathleen approached him while Fargo was checking his cinches and latigos. "Mr. Fargo, this delay troubles me. I open at the Bella Union on the twenty-first of this month. If we don't arrive in Santa Fe on the nineteenth, as scheduled, I won't even have time to recuperate from this horrid journey and attend dress rehearsal."

"I've got the nineteenth on my mind, too," Fargo assured her, "but for a different reason."

"I understand your meaning. So have I," she admitted. "I fear Lomax terribly. But the show must go on. We actors have our code, too."

Fargo turned the stirrup and swung up and over. "I respect that, lady. We can make up for lost time later, maybe, but those horses are damn near dead in the traces. There's no help for it—things are the way they are."

He touched his hat brim and gigged the Ovaro forward. Luck was with the travelers: less than a third of a mile ahead Fargo discovered a good spot in the lee of a small mesa, a circle of juniper trees with a small creek behind them. By the time the coach reached him and pulled off the trail, the last light had bled from the sky.

Fargo built a fire in a pit and put on a can of coffee to boil. He added his supply of hardtack and dried fruit to the last of Kathleen's hamper and a meager, somewhat odd meal was shared out.

"Booger and me will take turnabout on guard duty," Fargo remarked as he sipped from a tin cup of coffee. "But everybody stay alert. Keep a close eye on my horse—he's a crackerjack sentry. You won't catch Apaches sneaking in, but he's trained to alert at the Indian smell."

"I'll gladly take a stint of guard duty," Ashton said. "You two need your sleep, too."

Fargo shook his head. He had no proof against Ashton, but with Booger and Fargo both asleep, and the Ovaro available, it was too great a risk to trust him.

"'Preciate the offer," he said. "But me and Booger are drawing wages to get you folks through."

Trixie and Fargo had been exchanging coy glances in the flickering firelight. Booger noticed this and knew exactly what was on their minds. Now he watched Fargo from a sly, slanted, expectant glance. "Push-push," he whispered.

The preacher had been nervous and withdrawn since learning of the Apache menace. Now he spoke up.

"I fear it is God's will that we are all about to be slaughtered by the Godless red horde. I urge all of you to make peace with our Creator and ensure your place in His kingdom. No matter the weight of your sins, if—"

"Ease off that calamity howling," Fargo snapped, seeing the fearful look on the women's faces. "Just put some stiff in your spine, preacher. We're in a dirty corner, all right, but I've wangled out of worse."

"No, no, Fargo," Booger said, his tone conciliatory. "The skinny fellow with the big Bible is right—our time is at hand."

Booger had been visiting with his flask, and Fargo realized immediately that something sly was in the wind. He watched Booger heave to his feet and square off in front of a startled and puzzled Kathleen Barton.

"Your Loveliness, those who own souls may wish to heed the holy man. However, I am a pagan, as is Skye Fargo. I have always been Fargo's favorite gaffer—when there's dirty work, not fit for the lowest navvy, he sends for me. Well, pretty, this time he has got us both killed. So what is the point of cowardly indirection when men are about to die? On behalf of Fargo, myself, and these other three . . . men here gathered, I have a sincere request."

Oh, Christ, Fargo thought, knowing Booger's grift well enough to suspect where this was headed.

"And what might that be?" the curious actress inquired, perhaps expecting a request to perform one of her notable theatrical speeches.

Booger drew his massive bulk up formally. "For the reason I have just plainly spoke—our looming deaths—I'm after wondering: Is there the slightest chance at all of viewing your naked form before we die?"

Trixie was the first to react—she burst out laughing. "Booger, you aren't serious, are you?"

"Do you mean serious by nature, sweet britches? No . . . no, I would say that I'm quite gay, in the main. But I am a strapping big lad, and you know how we big fellows are happy by nature, having little to prove and all. And, of course, I'm hopeful that you, too, will shuck your clothing if Miss Barton will."

This was the first time Fargo had ever seen the actress look positively stupid.

"Now see here, fellow," Ashton interceded. "Keep a civil tongue in your head. That's quite enough of that."

"*Is* it, Latin man? Wouldn't *you* like to see her naked? Both of them?"

"That's not the—"

"You, stargazer?" Booger demanded of Malachi Feldman, whose embarrassed silence confessed for him.

Booger turned toward Brandenburg. "And you, holy man? No pious swamp gas, catfish. Don't *you* wunner what they look like stripped buck?"

"Sir, every man has his animal nature—"

"Ha-ho!" Booger exclaimed, looking at Kathleen. "The truth knocks him sick and silly. It's unanimous, America's Sweetheart. We who are about to die beseech you—strip."

Even in the firelight Fargo could tell her face was flaming. "You impertinent scoundrel!"

"Scoundrel, is it? You are the most beautiful woman in America. How am I a scoundrel for merely giving voice to a desire that every red-blooded man with a cod feels? What can be the harm?"

"Sew up your lips, Booger," Fargo snapped. "It was a nice try. But now you're humiliating the lady."

"Pah! *You're* the one who hinted you'd be under her petticoats before we reach Santa Fe—'the cat sits by the gopher hole,' you said."

Kathleen stared at Fargo, then back at Booger. "Apparently," she said, her tone brittle as skim ice, "I am trapped between the Scylla of arrogance and the Charybdis of vulgarity."

Booger looked to Fargo for a translation, but the Trails-man could only shrug.

"Sit down, Booger," Fargo said. "You flap your gums too much. You're an honest man but you don't have to say *every* damn thing that comes to your mind."

"It's the tormentin' itch, Fargo," Booger said sadly as he plopped down beside his friend. "The tormentin' itch." He leaned closer and whispered: "But as I promised you in El Paso: we *will* see her naked. Old Booger has his tricks."

There was an awkward silence after this bizarre farce. Fargo formed balls of cornmeal and water and tossed them into the hot ashes of the campfire to bake—corn dodgers for tomorrow's breakfast.

While he thus busied himself he listened to the reassuring insect hum, rising and falling like a person breathing. The indigo sky overhead was silver-peppered with a vast explosion of stars. To protect his night vision Fargo avoided gazing into the fire as the others were doing.

Instead, he watched the shape-changing shadows beyond the glow of the blood-orange flames. In this ancient land of Coronado, where foolish men chased golden chimeras called El Dorado and Cibola, Fargo always felt it—danger, yes, always, but also the ancient mystery and enchantment of New Mexico, where entire civilizations flourished and died centuries before the *Mayflower* was ever built.

Trixie's voice suddenly stirred him from his torpor like a slap to his face. "Well," she said, heading toward the coach, "I ain't about to waste that nice little creek. I'm gonna have me a bath. You coming, Miss Barton?"

The actress glowered at Booger. "After that lustful solilo-quy we just heard? I should think not. I may *add* clothing, not take any off."

Trixie rummaged in the boot of the Concord, then returned carrying a towel and a twisted knot of lye soap. Her eyes met Fargo's. "Suit yourself. Me, I can't wait to get out of these clothes. I just hope none of them Apaches sneak up on me—and me all alone back there."

Booger dug an elbow into Fargo's ribs. "Push-push."

"You go on and get in the water, Trixie," Fargo said. "I'll be along directly to make sure you're all right."

"How gallant, Sir Lancelot," Kathleen barbed.

"Oh, he lances a lot," Booger quipped, trying to keep his voice low and failing as usual.

"Yes," Kathleen agreed. "This will be his second . . . tournament in three days. Pity, isn't it, Mr. Fargo, that you'll have to wait until Santa Fe for any new conquests?"

"Oh, but the cat sits by the gopher hole," Booger reminded her.

"Scandalous," the preacher muttered. "And with wild savages all around us."

More awkward silence as the fire snapped and sparked. Soon a strong and pleasing voice—Trixie breaking out into trilling song as she bathed—reached them from the creek behind the trees:

French girls flirt with bold élan,
German girls cry, Danke schoen!
British gulls round their o's,
American gals cry, "Buy me clothes!"

Fargo was surprised to see this vigorous sally actually bring a twitch of smile to Kathleen's disdainful lips.

Skirts hitched up on spreading frame,
Petticoats are bright as flame,
Dainty high-heeled boots proclaim,
Fast Young Ladies!

"Why, she's really quite good," Kathleen murmured. "Truly talented."

She was indeed, Fargo thought. But Booger was right about the "tormentin' itch," and Fargo had been feeling it in spades ever since Trixie had whispered in his ear, back at San Marcial, "My naughty parts been tingling. I hope I'm next." He suspected her "talent" was varied.

Fargo threw the dregs of his coffee into the sand and stood up. "Guess I'll take a look around," he remarked casually.

"Yes, for after all you're drawing wages to protect us," Kathleen goaded, and Booger giggled like a half-wit.

Fargo did make a slow, vigilant circle of the campsite before going back to the creek. Generous moon wash, assisted by the brilliance of a heaven of stars, limned the arid landscape in an eerie, blue-white reflection. Rather than trying to spot Apaches—a bootless effort—he studied the ground for any tracks. All he found, however, were Trixie's prints and old tracks made by animals going to drink.

Fargo spotted Trixie as he rounded the circle of juniper trees, and his heart started pounding like fists on a drum. She stood in water up to her thighs, her ivory nudeness gleaming in the moonlight as she sudsed those firm, high-riding tits. When she stooped to rinse them off, turning halfway around to set her soap on the creek bank, her taut little Georgia-peach ass flexed even tighter.

"Damn, girl," Fargo called to her as he approached, "if you ain't a sight for sore eyes."

She whirled to watch him approach, walking stiffly from the force of his arousal. Her blond hair was done up in lovelocks with small curls water-plastered to her temples. But Fargo's eyes kept returning to those "gorgeous jahoobies" Booger worshipped with a passion—the sight of her there in the water egged on his lust, the erotic contrast posed by that delicate, thin frame supporting such huge globes.

"I wondered when you'd get here," she said breathlessly, taking a few steps toward him. Those exciting tits swayed with real ocean motion, huge, heavy swells. "C'mon in."

Fargo grounded his Henry, shucked his shell belt, and waded into the cool water. Trixie cupped her tits as if offering them to him and Fargo was in no dickering mood. He crouched and took first one, then the other nipple into his hungry mouth, licking and sucking them stiff.

She urged him on in a voice melodic as waltzing violins. "Nibble a little too, wouldja, Skye? Just little fish nibbles? That gets me so—*ohh*, yes, like *that*!"

By now Fargo was hot as a branding iron, and his man gland was straining for release. That's exactly what Trixie had in mind, too, as she fumbled his fly open and went down on her knees.

"That damn Booger won't give us much time 'fore he

sneaks down here," she whispered, "so I'm gonna do what I been wantin' to since I seen your hard pizzle."

Tight, wet heat flowed over Fargo's length as she took as much of him as she could into her eager mouth. Her head pistoned back and forth, faster and faster, fueled by the fire of lust raging inside her. The way she tightened her lips and cheeks on him—grip and release, grip and release—made Fargo feel as if his manhood were sheathed in a snug velvet glove that had come to life.

It didn't take much of this treatment before Fargo felt himself swelling drumhead tight. He suddenly groaned like a man in pain, erupting over and over until his weak legs folded and he collapsed to his knees in the water, dazed and panting.

"Before you leave Santa Fe, Skye," her hot whisper tickled his ear, "can I feel that big, beautiful thing inside me?"

"Hell, yes," he replied, "unless we can wangle a way to do it sooner. Matter fact"—he guided her hand downward—"feels like he's already angry again. Why'n't we—"

Just then, however, Fargo heard the long, ululating howl of a coyote, ending on a series of yipping barks.

The favorite signal of Apaches prowling in the dark.

"Get dressed quick," Fargo told her. "Our fun is going to have to wait."

June fifteenth dawned hot and still, a breezeless morning with an ominous feel to it that set Fargo's teeth on edge. He had slept very little the night before, even when Booger spelled him in two-hour rotations. But the expected attack did not come.

A full night's rest, with grain and plenty of water, had put some fettle back in the horses. Booger's whip was already cracking soon after sunrise.

"We can get this rig to La Joya by noon," Booger predicted, "unless Red John takes a fancy to hit us sooner."

Fargo studied the terrain through his field glasses. This stretch, between the Rio Grande to the west and the Los Pinos mountains to the east, was mostly desolate and flat, wiry patches of *palomilla* and the occasional cholla cactus the only terrain features. But it was also crisscrossed by deep arroyos, desert ditches formed over centuries by sudden downpours. For raiding Indians these provided a hidden network of attack trails that kept them below the horizon until just before an attack.

"It won't be beer and skittles after La Joya, either," Fargo pointed out. "Red Sash and his Jicarilla renegades could hit us anytime between here and just south of Albuquerque. That's why I'd just as soon have the frolic now. Lomax's yellow dogs will be on our spoor again soon enough, and I'm for shaking these Apaches off us now."

"The hell *you* bawlin' about?" Booger demanded. "*You* got pussy last night. Old Booger's gonna die with a dry dick. Gerlong!" he shouted at the team, tickling the leaders with his whip.

Hundreds of miles of stagecoach driving without relief showed clearly in Booger's slack, exhausted face and cracked lips. The unrelenting Southwest sun, the swirling billows of eye-galling dust, even the constant fatigue of controlling the reins exacted a harsh toll and would have left most drivers prostrate by now.

"I don't like this," Fargo said a few minutes later, watching a point about two miles to the northeast. "We got no wind, but there's a dust haze coming at us. I can't spot any riders though."

"Arroyos," Booger said grimly, snatching his North & Savage from its buckskin sheath. "Them Apaches can move around like moles."

"Get set for a dustup!" Fargo called down to the passengers. "Stay below the windows. If any fire arrows hit the coach, it's up to you men to jerk 'em out if you can reach 'em."

"Moses on the mountain!" Booger exclaimed. "Here they are to open the ball!"

The desiccated earth suddenly seemed to be spitting out Apaches as they debouched from an arroyo only a mile or so east of the stage. Fargo recognized the distinctive red headbands of the Apache and, as they rode closer, the deep chests and powerfully muscled arms that set them apart from the rest of the mostly slender-limbed Plains warriors. Most had rifles raised high in one hand, a few others red-streamered lances or iron-bladed battle axes traded from the slave-trading *Comancheros*.

"I was right," Fargo said. "I count twenty. Some are riding big cavalry sorrels, some mustangs. Doesn't look like they plan to charge right off. The one with the copper brassards on his arms must be Red Sash—he's carrying the medicine shield."

"Them mother-humpin' Apaches like to play with their food," Booger said. "They'll likely pace us for a time to scare the snot outta the passengers and unstring our nerves. All the time, they squeeze in gradual like, then—whoop!— they'll commence to shrieking and attack us full bore."

"That's the way of it," Fargo agreed. "But they expect me to be armed with the usual express gun. They don't know we got Mr. Henry's magazine repeater on board, the gun you load on Sunday and fire all week. To hell with waiting for the attack, old son. Soon's they close in a few hundred yards closer, I plan to start kissing the mistress."

Fargo rolled atop the coach and took up a spread-legged prone position. He kept his Henry down out of sight, deliberately letting the sawed-off double-ten show.

Dust spiraled up as the Apaches gradually reined their mounts closer, riding in a long skirmish line that would form into a flying wedge once they attacked—unlike most tribes, the adaptable Apaches emulated the tactics of their American and Mexican enemies.

"Can't this coach go any faster?" the preacher shouted out the window. "God bless us, they're getting closer!"

"Caulk up, you white-livered, chicken-gutted psalm singer!" Booger shouted back. "Why'n't you quit huggin' that damn Bible and read us something from it? I like that part where Joseph ties his ass to a tree and proceeds to Bethlehem. Musta had India-rubber hinders in them days, huh?"

"You blaspheming bully! May you roast in hellfire!"

"And may you die of the runny shits, you horse-faced whelp of an unbaptized whore!"

Fargo laughed out loud, shaking his head. "Booger, you are some piece of work."

"Upon my word, Fargo, that half-faced goat better pray he dies today. Happens he don't, Old Booger will be wearing his guts for garters."

Still Fargo waited, letting the Apaches close into better range. He wasn't sure his strategy of sudden, quick, surprise kills would work with this tribe. Northern tribes believed in strict gods who placed great value on the holiness of an Indian's life—thus most battle leaders called for retreat after the loss of one or two braves.

But the Apaches, tempered hard by their harsh environment and constant warfare to stay alive, believed in a more remote god called Great Ussen. Ussen was mainly seen as natural forces such as the power of motion in the wind. Thus, steep battle losses did not confer holy disfavor.

"All right!" Fargo called down to Booger. "I'm opening up on them. Stay frosty and shoot plumb. They'll try to spread out and get to our left flank for a pincers. I want you to drop only horses, Booger. We can't let them get close enough to kill our team."

Fargo had to combine accuracy with speed and fully exploit the element of surprise. He dropped a bead on the last rider in the skirmish line, and the Henry kicked into his shoulder when he knocked him from the saddle. Rapidly firing and levering, he worked his way up the line. In the ten seconds or so that it took the Jicarillas to realize they were up against a dead aim with an excellent repeating rifle, Fargo had killed or wounded five Apaches.

Booger, meantime, had opened up with his North & Savage. His sitting, offhand position and slower weapon made him less effective, but he sent three horses buckling, further weakening Red Sash's battle group before the surprised Apaches even got off a shot.

However, the battle-hardened warriors recovered quickly, and their excellent marksmanship made retribution swift and punishing. They opened fire with a vengeance, shrill war cries punctuating their coup de main.

"Here's the fandango!" Fargo sang out cheerfully as a flurry of slugs and flint-tipped arrows peppered the coach.

A moving target was harder to hit, and Booger kept the coach in swift motion, alternately whipping the team and returning fire. Fargo, down to eleven loads in his Henry, fired more selectively. He hit fewer braves as the Apaches resorted to their defensive riding patterns and lowered their target profiles.

"Oh, Jesus, I've been shot!" Malachi Feldman's voice screeched like a hog under the blade.

"Calm down, you hysterical fool!" Ashton shouted, and there was a hard slapping sound from the coach. "You've just been creased! Cover the women!"

"God preserve us!" the preacher's voice added to the pandemonium.

A bullet thwacked into the coach, tossing splinters into Fargo's face. He still had eight shots in the Henry's tube magazine when a casing suddenly jammed in the ejector port. Knowing from experience it would take at least twenty seconds to carefully pry it out with the tip of his knife, and with several braves now in easy range and closing fast, Fargo cursed and tossed the weapon aside.

Booger was down to his dragoon pistol, the big weapon leaping in his fist. To keep the lead flying, Fargo shucked out his Colt and made six quick, successive snap-shots. Horses would have been easier targets, but he knew the Apaches probably had plenty of remounts. It was manpower he had to deplete to quell any future attacks, so Fargo targeted riders.

He and Booger wiped two more renegades from their sheepskin-pad saddles, but the Apache return fire was more deadly now, and suddenly the nearside swing horse slumped dead in the traces, dragging the coach to a stop.

Fargo knew they had reached the crisis point, and at first all seemed lost. Fargo had depleted his spare cylinder, too, and despite having killed or wounded more than half the attackers, he and Booger had no time to reload. A movement in the corner of his eye made Fargo glance toward the rear of the coach just in the nick of time to spot Red Sash with his knife cocked back to throw—in the desperate confusion, he had managed to ride around on the south flank and leap onto the coach.

Fargo rolled hard and fast as Red Sash threw his knife, grabbing the express gun and cocking both hammers. Sprawled on his back, Fargo fired both barrels almost point-blank. The twin load of buckshot lifted the Apache off the coach in a bloody spray. Seeing their battle leader land in an ungainly heap behind the swift wagon shocked the rest and broke the back of their attack. They scattered to the east like dogs with their tails on fire.

When the smoke cleared, the stink of saltpeter and death was thick in the broiling heat. Fargo, his face blackened with powder, sat up and thumbed reloads into his Colt as he watched the Apaches retreat. The sudden calm, after a pitched battle, always seemed eerie to him.

"You hit, Booger?"

"Not so's you'd notice. Think them red Arabs will mount a vengeance raid?"

"No. This bunch are after loot, not coup feathers. But I'll still feel better when we clear out of here. They'll be back to get their dead—or at least their weapons."

Fargo raised his voice. "You folks all right down there?"

"Malachi got nicked in his ribs, Skye," Trixie answered, a tremble in her voice. "But it's piddlin'. Laws! I thought sure we was all goners!"

"Stay put," Fargo said. "We got to switch out a dead horse, then we're pulling foot."

"Fargo," Booger said just before both men climbed down, "have I thanked you yet for naming old Booger as your driver on this run? My only regret is that I will not leave a widow for you to fuck after you get me killed."

"That is a shame," Fargo agreed. "You got any sisters?"

11

Russ Alcott lowered his spyglass and loosed a sharp whistle. "Boys, that's what you call painting the landscape with blood. Them was Apaches they just routed, and them red sons ain't no cracker-and-molasses Injins. *Two* of 'em whipped a force that was ten to one against 'em."

Alcott, Cleo Hastings and Spider Winslowe were well hidden in a river thicket beside the Rio Grande. Alcott, picking his teeth with a twig, was silent for a full minute, thinking hard.

"Well, that flat out does it," he finally announced. "It's open country ahead and we ain't got a snowball's chance to kill Fargo and snatch that woman anytime before they hit Albuquerque."

"Why don't we give Fargo the go-by and just grab the woman?" Spider suggested.

"You been grazin' locoweed? Fargo's a jobber and his job right now is to protect that pert skirt. Even if we could do it, it's no use taking her withouten we kill Fargo. They say he can hold a trail in windstorms that blow even insect tracks away. We'd never shake him."

Thus reined in by logic, Spider tried another tack. "What about the station at Peralta just south of Albuquerque? Maybe we could—"

Alcott waved this off. "Nah, we'd just be barkin' at a knot. We bollixed it up back at San Marcial and now Fargo will be on guard at the stations. Good ambush country starts just past Rio Rancho. I use to ride with Jack Dancy's gang up that way; I know the country good."

"Yeah, Russ, but hell," Spider protested. "This is already the fifteenth of June. By the time they hit Rio Rancho, it'll be the seventeenth before we can make another play. That gives us only three days—ain't that paring the cheese might close to the rind?"

"What cheese?" Cleo put in, confused, but the other two ignored him.

"*Too* damn close," Alcott agreed. "But, see, we got us another problem in the mix—that goddamn driver."

"Yeah. 'At sumbitch is a big grizz, ain't he?"

"Size ain't nothing to the matter, Spider. That bastard is crazy-brave, and that's the worst kind. Just now—bullets was humming in nineteen to the dozen, and did you *see* him laughing while them Apaches attacked? Hell, he enjoyed it. We ain't never gonna whip the pair of 'em together."

"You mean we're just gonna give up?" Cleo demanded.

Alcott gave him a pitying look. "*Here's* a man knows gee from haw," he replied scornfully. "When you ever seen Russ Alcott get icy boots? I'm just telling you, lunkhead, we got to kill the big grizz *first* if we want even odds at Fargo."

"Sure," Spider said, "but how we gonna play a deal like that?"

"I ain't got a foggy notion in hell," Alcott admitted. "Unless . . ."

"Unless what?"

"Unless," Alcott said, thinking out loud more than speaking, "we can maybe rub him out in Albuquerque. That's an Overland stagecoach hub and more in the way of a saloon than a station house. Spider, are you still in thick with that pretty Mex'can whore, what's-her-name?"

"Conchita? Sure, I trimmed her just before we took this job. She's the one helped me kill Billy Hanchon. That hot little twat will do anything for a gold double eagle."

"She still got her that crib right along the river behind Albuquerque station?"

Spider nodded. A sudden spark of hope animated Alcott's pale-ice eyes.

"Now we're cookin', boys! That big son of a bitch siding Fargo is bad trouble, all right, but he ain't got the think-piece Fargo's got. And he drinks whiskey like he's a pipe through the floor—I seen him at San Marcial. The main mile is to get him away from Fargo long enough to kill him. We're gonna ride hard and talk to this little Mexer. That coach will pull into Albuquerque sometime late tomorrow, and we're gonna make damn sure it pulls out with a different driver."

On June sixteenth, two hours before sunset, Fargo watched the adobe and red-tile buildings of Albuquerque heave into view ahead of them.

Nestled between the Rio Grande and the Sandia Mountains, the dusty frontier outpost had, in the era of New Spain, served merely as a layover for caravans traveling the long trade route known as El Camino Real—the King's Highway—linking Santa Fe with Chihuahua, Durango, Aguascalientes and other interior cities of Mexico. Recently, however, it had become a transportation center for people and goods throughout the American Southwest.

The sight seemed to stir Booger from a hibernation state brought on by exhaustion. "My favorite station, Fargo! Good eats, cheap tarantula juice, and the best-lookin' sparkling doxies in Zeb Pike's wasteland. Old Booger will finally get himself a spot of the old in-out, hey?"

"Don't go treating the place like Fiddler's Green," Fargo warned. "We shook the Apaches off our tails, but we've still got Zack Lomax's curly wolves looking to put us with our ancestors. Go easy on the whiskey, and keep your eyes to all sides."

"Faugh! Them jackleg gunmen will catch a weasel asleep before they surprise *this* child."

A half hour later the Concord pulled in at Overland's big wagon yard. Unlike the sleep station at Peralta, the place was a hive of activity. The big depot wasn't very impressive from the outside, even drowning in burnished-gold sunlight as it was now. Departing from the rest of the town's architecture, it was a low, split-slab building with a shake roof and a long tie-rail out front still covered with bark. Nearly transparent hides had been stretched over the windows to keep out the grit-laden winds that plagued Albuquerque.

The inside, however, was bright and cheery, the plastered walls turned into painted murals depicting red rock canyons and pristine mountain ranges. The building was divided into a cluster of small sleeping rooms for children and female passengers and a bustling cantina that, like the relaxed public standards in Santa Fe, was open to both sexes.

"Where is the ladies' bathhouse?" Kathleen demanded the moment the travelers from El Paso entered the depot.

Fargo bit his lower lip to keep from grinning. "Sorry, lady, but water scarcity plagues this town. Spring runoff from the mountains was low this year, and they'll barely have enough for the horses."

"Drat!" She stamped her foot in frustration. "Half the dust from the trail seems to have settled on me."

Trixie caught Fargo's eye. "You should have bathed in that creek where we camped, Miss Barton. It was real nice."

"Oh, I wouldn't want to have ruined your fun—or Mr. Fargo's."

Trixie shrugged. "Don't bother me if people watch. They might learn something."

"Disgraceful," Pastor Brandenburg muttered. "Modesty is a virtue, Miss Belle, as is purity."

"What about hypocrisy?" Ashton asked the preacher. "You'd give anything to have been in Fargo's place. An honest pagan is better than a bad Catholic."

"Now, now, Your Loftiness," Booger soothed Kathleen, who was still petulant. "No need to fret. Old Booger gives you his word you will have a fine, hot bath when we reach San Felipe."

"Oh? Another water trough, I suppose?"

Booger glanced at Fargo and winked. "No cruel jokes this time. A fine bathhouse just for the ladies. Plenty of privacy."

"I'm famished," Malachi Feldman complained. "Let's get some hot food."

Despite the number of female passengers in the cantina, the place had the grim, masculine smell of any other frontier saloon: sweat, unwashed bodies, tobacco and pungent liquor. Fargo stepped through the archway ahead of the others and took a careful look around. Then he waved the rest in.

A big Navajo wearing a red plume in his low-crowned leather hat was tending bar, and Fargo noticed several dark-skinned Mexicans with flashing white teeth and dark, dangerous eyes—eyes that fastened appreciatively on the two women as they entered.

Trixie wrinkled her nose at the stench of heavy Mexican tobacco, stronger even than cigar smoke. "These Spaniards look like some rough fellows," she remarked nervously.

"Pah!" Booger scoffed. "Ol' Sancho likes to flash a knife, but it's like they say about the Espanish navy: 'A frog likes his cognac, a limey his rum, but the dago sticks to port.'"

Kathleen noticed how Fargo stayed close to her side and did not relax his vigilance.

"I certainly feel well protected," she remarked, a note of sarcasm seeping into her tone. "I suppose next you will insist on sleeping in my room?"

"I hate to disappoint you," Fargo replied, "but Booger and me have already agreed to take turns sitting in a chair *outside* your door."

They settled at an empty table and Booger gathered up the meal chits, taking them back to the kitchen. Kathleen had been watching a number of young women—smoke-eyed women who flirted from behind palmetto fans—enticing male travelers.

"Well, Mr. Fargo," she taunted, "they all certainly notice you. Perhaps you'll make that third conquest after all?"

"It's not really a conquest," Fargo explained, "if a man pays for it."

"Oh? Something *you* never resort to, I'm sure."

"Why would I when there's plenty of volunteers?"

"Yes, you are a ruggedly handsome fellow, I suppose. But, of course, men who wear bloody buckskins and carry knives in their boots are perforce limited to women of easy virtue—women who make little distinction between a bed and a berry patch."

Ashton snickered, Trixie frowned, the preacher clutched his Bible tighter. Feldman, busy untying a chamois pouch, seemed not to have heard. Fargo held the actress's gaze and replied amiably, "Generally they forget real quick where they are. And I've found that a woman who's good in bed is usually even better on the floor."

Kathleen flushed just as Booger returned with a bottle of red-eye and a tray of pony glasses. "Grub pile in just a few minutes. No beans this time, Miss Barton."

She flushed even deeper. But by now Booger had shifted

his attention to Feldman. "H'ar now, you little pop-eyed freak. What's that in your pouch?"

"The world-famous traveling moon pebbles, Mr. McTeague."

"No Choctaw here, catfish."

"It's not Choctaw, it's plain English. I assume you are aware that millions of birds migrate to the moon every winter?"

"Teach your grandmaw to suck eggs."

"It's scientific fact," Feldman insisted. "Surely, at night, you've seen geese flying into the face of the moon. It is only a few hundred miles from Earth and easily reached by most birds."

Booger looked a question at Fargo. The Trailsman, by a supreme effort, kept a straight face. "I have heard," he replied truthfully, "that birds can fly to the moon."

"Indeed they can," Feldman said, warming to his theme. "And some of them bring back moon pebbles in their beaks. Pebbles like these."

He shook out six round, gray objects the size of marbles and formed a circle with them on the table. Booger finished his whiskey and wiped his mouth on his sleeve, staring at them. "Pah! Them could be kidney stones passed by a bull moose for aught I know."

"No, sir. These moon pebbles are distinct, for unlike any pebbles found on Earth they are animate—they can travel on their own."

He reached into the pouch again and produced a "pebble" twice the size of the others. "All they require is a leader stone. The moment they sense the presence of a leader, they immediately travel to it—safety in numbers and all that."

He placed the largest pebble in the center of the circle. Booger started, his eyes widening, when the six smaller pebbles instantly rolled inward until tightly clustered around the large one.

"Carry me out!" he exclaimed. "Carry me out with tongs! Them sons-a-bitches scuttled like bugs! Fargo, you seen that too?"

"Sure did," Fargo replied.

"Well, old Booger is clemmed! I'll allow I never seen the

like in all my born days! Say, little fellow, what will you take for them?"

Trixie, unable to hold off any longer, sputtered with laughter but disguised it as a cough. Even Kathleen, Fargo noticed, was actually smiling.

"McTeague," Lansford Ashton said, "have you never heard of magnets?"

He suddenly brought a fist down hard on one of the pebbles. It disintegrated to a white powder, revealing a small piece of metal within. "These 'pebbles' are merely plaster of paris painted gray. The biggest one has a magnet inside."

"Ignore this skeptic, Mr. McTeague," Feldman spoke up quickly. "I might be persuaded to part with these rare objects for—"

Booger cut him off with a growl, his face bloated with anger. "Walk your chalk, you filthy bedlamite, or I'll pump a bullet into your bagpipes. You think old Booger don't know sic 'em about magnates? Why, I spotted your grift all along."

"Magnets," Fargo corrected him. "Not magnates."

"Hey, Booger," Trixie cut in, "I got some pieces of wood that can square-dance. Wanna buy 'em?"

Booger scowled and poured more whiskey while everyone except Kathleen and the dour-faced preacher laughed. Fargo, however, closely watched a pretty Mexican soiled dove who had not taken her attention off Booger since he arrived, her eyes watching him through the black lace mantilla over her head.

Kathleen saw Fargo watching the girl and mistook his interest. "Surely, Mr. Fargo, she's a mercenary. Or perhaps you think even a pretty adventuress will dally with you gratis?"

"Take a closer look. It's not me she's eyeballing."

Kathleen did look. "Yes . . . yes, I see what you mean. Well, I suppose Mr. McTeague is an easy sale. He's already drunk."

"Could be," Fargo said. "But there's plenty of other men in here I'd pick first if I was a sporting girl."

Kathleen suddenly caught his drift. "You don't mean . . . ?"

"Lomax's men? Why not? Booger is obnoxious, foul-mouthed, and generally acts like a fool. But he's hell on two sticks when the war whoop sounds. They must know that by now, and maybe they figure they'll never get to me—and you—until they put him under."

Fargo quickly turned the problem over with the fingers of his mind the way a jeweler might study facets of a stone. The more he looked, the worse it smelled.

The Mexican girl made her move, stopping by Booger's chair and whispering something in his ear. She headed for the door and Booger rose to follow her. Fargo caught up with him halfway to the door.

"Let it go, Booger. That gal's been paid to lure you out."

Booger, his moon face flush with drink, narrowed his eyes in suspicion. "H'ar now! You have *your* ration of free cunny, eh? But old Booger may not even *pay* for it? Fargo, like I warned you: I'm a volcano fixin' to explode. Gangway or I'll dust your doublet!"

"Let it go, hoss. All that's waiting for you is a lead bath."

"Pah! Acknowledge the corn, Fargo—you're jealous because she prefers a big brute like me over you. Say! One love bite hides another, hey? Let's go tandem on her and then flip to see who pays."

"Booger, c'mon back inside. I give you my word: when we get to Santa Fe you can have all the frippet you want and I'll post the pony."

"Clean your ears or cut your hair, catfish. Never come twixt a dog and his meat."

Booger swept Fargo aside with one brawny arm, almost knocking him ass-over-applecart. Fargo cursed, knowing he couldn't stop the horny giant without shooting him. He turned and glanced quickly around the cantina. A man wearing the five-pointed star of a deputy sheriff stood hip-cocked at the bar, conversing with another man. Fargo quickly crossed the cantina.

"Ask you a favor, deputy?" Fargo greeted him.

The lawman's suspicious eyes traveled the stranger's length. "And just what might that be, Mr. . . . ?"

"Fargo. Skye Fargo. You see that beautiful woman waiting for her supper at the table in the center of the room?"

"See her? I ain't looked at much else since you folks come in. Skye Fargo, you say? Aren't you—"

"I'm her bodyguard," Fargo cut him off. "That's Kathleen Barton, the actress. Her life's been threatened, but right now I have to step out back. Would you go sit in that chair beside her until I get back?"

The deputy grinned and pushed away from the bar. "Does a whore take a quick bath? I just placed your name, Trailsman. Take your time outside, but make damn sure the bullet hole ain't in the back—Sheriff Kinney don't like that."

Fargo hurried outside into the darkness. He rounded a corner of the depot and spotted a row of whores' cribs—a half-dozen makeshift, clapboard huts with blankets for doors and no windows—down near the river. Moonlight was generous enough to show that no one was lurking out in front of them.

There . . . there was a wide chink in the back of the third crib through which oily yellow light spilled out. Enough light to show the outline of a man's face peering inside. A moment later Fargo heard the faint, familiar click of a hammer being cocked.

Quicker than thought he filled his hand with blue steel. "Drop that thumb-buster, mister, *now*, or you'll be shoveling coal in hell."

That was more warning than a cold-blooded murderer deserved, but Fargo hoped to beat some information out of the scut. However, that plan went to hell when the man whirled and fired at him, the bullet passing so close to Fargo's head that he felt the wind-rip from it.

His Colt bucked in his fist, there was a sound like a hammer hitting a watermelon, and the mystery assassin flumped to the ground. It took his nervous system a few seconds to accept the fact of death—by the time Fargo reached him, the dead man's heels finally quit scratching at the ground like frantic claws.

Booger, who even in the throes of alcohol and lust reacted instantly to trouble, was at Fargo's side when the Trailsman scratched a lucifer to life. Fargo's bullet had punctured the left lung and possibly nicked the heart. The man died with the surprised, betrayed stare of death etched onto his face, pink froth speckling his lips. The last wisp of smoke still curled from his Remington muzzle like an undulating snake.

"Recognize him?" Fargo asked, staring at the bland, smooth-shaven face.

"Only as the Grim Reaper," Booger replied. "Fargo, you saved old Booger's life—give us a kiss."

"No you don't!" Fargo leaped a few feet to safety, in no mood to get the air crushed out of him.

"Conchita! That treacherous little whore," Booger said, staring at the crib. "Why, I've a mind to—"

"Ease off," Fargo said. "She likely did it for money, but you know a soiled dove is powerless if men threaten her. They can't go to the law. Besides, if we treat her right we might get some information."

Booger mulled this and then nodded. "Right as rain, Fargo. Old Booger will feel bad later if he beats the shit out of a woman."

"Now you're whistling. We'll talk to her before we leave Albuquerque. Hey—where you going?"

"Back inside to finish what I started. The little bitch will never charge me now, and Mrs. McTeague's boy Booger never passes up free poon."

12

Jim Hargrove, the Albuquerque deputy Fargo had approached in the cantina, recognized the corpse instantly.

"Congratulations, Fargo, on a job well done. You just killed Spider Winslowe, one of the most wanted hombres in the territory. He's a murderer and road agent. Had him his own gang up around Santa Fe."

The match blew out and both men stood up.

"I recognize the name," Fargo said. "Didn't troops out of Fort Union bust up the gang?"

"Yeah, 'bout six months back. Two were killed, one's in prison and will soon be dancing on air. But Winslowe escaped and hit the owlhoot trail. Nobody knows what the hell he's been up to since then. Why's he trying to kill you and McTeague?"

"Just clearing the path so he can get at the actress. I think I've also butted heads with one of the murdering jackals with him. Handsome, clean-cut type with a mean mouth. Rides a roan and wears fancy silver spurs. He's got eyes that look like they were chipped off a block of ice."

"Christ, that sounds like Russ Alcott. Gunslinger. Far as I know he's not officially on the dodge, but that son of a bitch has depopulated half of Lincoln County. And he's smart as a steel trap. If that lead-chucker is in the mix, you're up against it, Fargo. Try to avoid a draw-shoot—he can clear leather today and kill a man yesterday."

Later, as he sat guard outside Kathleen Barton's door, Fargo sent Booger to fetch Conchita. As Fargo expected, she neither could nor would tell him anything Deputy Hargrove hadn't already told him. However, after he slipped her a quarter-eagle gold piece, she confirmed having seen Winslowe and Alcott together recently.

"There's at least one other man in on it," Fargo told Booger after the soiled dove had gone. "That face watching me from the hotel window in El Paso had a big, droopy teamster's mustache. But that's all I noticed, and it's worthless—that kind of lip whisker is common on the frontier."

"To me," Booger scoffed, "my enemy is any needle-dick bug fucker who tries to shoot me. Who gives two hoots in hell what his name is? Hell, we ain't serving warrants."

"True, you ugly flea-hive, but I'm worried about Zack Lomax, assuming he's the ramrod of this plot to kill Kathleen. If I only get her safely to Santa Fe, then drop it like it's none of my business, her life is forfeit. So what if he misses the June nineteenth deadline? He likely figures it's better to kill her late than never. I need all the proof I can get that he's tied to Alcott and the others."

"Proof! Faugh! If you're talking help from the law, Fargo, you're searching for a will-o'-the-wisp. America's Sweetheart or no, Lomax is likely a rich toff—them bastards spread money around like manure, and a lawman is easy bought. Happens you want that highfalutin bitch to be safe, *we'll* hafta kill Lomax."

Fargo nodded. "Even more reason why I require proof. I don't kill any man until I'm convinced he *requires* killing."

"Why, you squeamish little Quaker! I say kill 'em all and let God sort 'em out."

Booger relieved Fargo at two a.m. and the Trailsman caught a few hours of uneasy sleep in the bunkhouse for male passengers. Because they had lost time farther south, Fargo insisted on pulling out as soon as the sun cleared the horizon.

Malachi Feldman was about to step into the coach when he abruptly exclaimed, "Saints preserve us!"

"What's your grift now?" Ashton snapped.

"Sir, it has nothing to do with me. There's no mistaking the celestial signs. Look at the sky, all of you! See it? The sun and a full moon, both visible in the sky simultaneously. A bloodred sun and a pale-ghost moon. The Eighth House is ascendant and we are *all* doomed! This is a death coach!"

"Give over with such balderdash," Pastor Brandenburg said impatiently. "Man proposes but God disposes."

"Then may He dispose of both of you," Booger scoffed from up on the box. "Neither one of you yahoos knows beans from buckshot."

"Malachi knows plaster of paris from pebbles," Fargo taunted and Booger shook a fist under his nose. A moment later, however, both men broke out laughing.

"Aye, that little pip-squeak made a monkey of me," Booger admitted. "The cunning bastard—if he had a set on him he'd be a good horse thief. Gerlong there, boys! G'long!"

However, as they rolled out of the big yard, Booger cracking his blacksnake, Fargo wasn't all that convinced that Malachi's "celestial sign" was pure balderdash. Fargo had never been a big believer in "portents," but just before Lansford Ashton boarded the Concord he had met Fargo's eyes and held them for a long moment. And again Fargo had recalled his strange dream just before the explosion at San Marcial: a silver concho belt turning into a snake with bloody fangs.

No, Fargo placed no great importance on portents. But sometimes, he reminded himself, it was wise to heed the signs, whether on a trail or in a dream.

When he was particularly agitated, Zack Lomax would retire to a back room of his College Street mansion and vigorously lift sandbags to work off his nervous tension. By late in the forenoon of June seventeenth he was indeed agitated— his special messenger had just left after delivering the latest mirror-relay report from Russ Alcott.

"Spider's been killed," he reported to his lackey Olney Lucas. "Gunned down last night by Fargo. Only three days left, Olney, and my careful plan is in danger of unraveling."

Lomax lay on a folded quilt, repeatedly pressing a sandbag out to arm's length from his chest. "Three goddamn days, Olney, and no progress!"

"You have to stay frosty, boss," Olney soothed him. He had seen Lomax like this before, when the "controlled madness" of his personality threatened to shade over into sheer, unpredictable insanity. "Remember, these past few days that

105

stagecoach has been in wide-open country. But they're north of Albuquerque now. The route veers out of the river valley and bends east toward Santa Fe. Timbered ridges, red rock canyons—prime ambush country."

Lomax appeared not to have heard him. He continued furiously pumping the sandbag up and down, sweat pouring off his face.

"Fargo!" Lomax's mouth twisted bitterly around the word. "A true-blue, blown-in-the-bottle legend. The trouble with a legend, Olney, is that the legend eventually becomes the man. Russ isn't afraid of Fargo—his nerves are unstrung by the power of the legend."

"It's not just legend, boss. They've made three attempts on Fargo and failed each time—and now Spider's dead. It was Fargo who killed him, not the legend."

"Yes, Spider. That's bad for me, too. By now Fargo no doubt knows who Spider Winslowe was. That brings him one step closer to finding out that Cort Bergman, respectable Santa Fe mining consultant, is actually Zack Lomax."

This was true and Olney knew it also brought Skye Fargo one step closer to finding out about *him*—the man who was assisting Lomax in a plot to kill the most popular woman in America. And any woman killer, in the West, would never even live to be hanged. Olney screwed up his courage to speak.

"Boss? What boots it to lick old wounds?"

"What's that?" Lomax said absently, finally setting the sandbag aside and sitting up.

"This plan of yours, I mean. All right, the bitch gelded you in public. But, hell, you're a rainmaker. You got a good deal going here in Santa Fe. Fine house and money to toss at the birds. Why risk losing all that? You can kill her easy once she gets here and Fargo leaves town—it doesn't *have* to be on the nineteenth while he's still around."

He steeled himself for an explosion of rage. But Lomax only sat stone still, his normally incandescent eyes now gloomy with speculation.

"No, Olney," he replied in a tone of quiet menace, "it *must* be done my way. You can't understand that because you are merely a practical man with the usual motivations.

Kathleen Barton has a blood reckoning coming. I must have my way in this or else that vicious bitch's victory over me will plague me to my deathbed like a bastard child."

Again he fell into brooding reverie, his face tightening and contorting as memory replayed that unspeakable humiliation of nearly a year ago. Finally:

"Olney," he said energetically, stirring himself back to the problem at hand, "I still have an ace up my sleeve, and it's riding on that coach right now. Tomorrow we flash the signal to Russ: he's going to join forces, if necessary, with my passenger. The key will be a well-coordinated move during the last legs from Domingo to Santa Fe. Toward that end I'll be sending you on another errand. In the meantime, however, Russ and Cleo must keep trying on their own. Time is a bird and the bird is on the wing."

Lomax stood up, those intense, burning eyes forcing Olney to avert his gaze. "Living legends, like everyone else, have to die. I *will* kill that ball-breaking slut on June nineteenth, and that means Fargo dies first. We've got three whole days, and death takes less than a second."

By late afternoon of June seventeenth the Concord coach had reached the rolling timberland north of Bernalillo. To the west the Rio Grande was still visible through breaks in the towering pines, but the Overland Stage road was gradually meandering farther out of the safety of the valley and into blue, spruce-covered hills. A westering sun threw long, flat shadows to the east.

"Stay sharp now," Fargo warned Booger. "Alcott and whoever's siding him could dry-gulch us anytime now."

"You see any green on my antlers?" Booger shot back. "You think old Booger ain't never been up against it before?"

Fargo noted the snappish irritation in his friend's tone—not his usual gait. Fargo also noticed the slack, glazed look to his face and felt a quick stab of guilt. He had insisted, in El Paso, that Booger make the entire run to Santa Fe. Now Fargo regretted that demand—exhaustion was clearly exacting a high toll from the driver.

"Hell, Booger, that's why I wouldn't make this run without you. I knew I couldn't do it without a stout lad like you. I can't think of a better man to ride the river with. You're all grit and a yard wide."

"No need to slop over," Booger grumped, looking highly pleased. "And I'm a bit *over* a yard wide, catfish."

Fargo grinned even as his weather-tanned face turned again to the prime ambush country east of the trail. His Henry lay across his thighs now, and he kept his sun-crimped eyes in constant motion. He lowered his voice.

"I notice you ain't too sweet on Lansford Ashton," he remarked. "What's your size-up on him?"

Booger shook his head and spat a brown streamer, his usual gesture of contempt for all the world's fools, knaves and villains.

"He's got the Latin look, Skye—*pig* Latin. That spade-bearded bastard would steal a hot stove and come back for the smoke. He's one a them sons-a-bitches who sits in front of a warm fire all winter, profiting off another man's hunger and toil and blood."

"You're a pretty good judge of human nature, old son, but I don't think he spends much time sitting in front of fires. He's got go muscles on him and hard hands—I'd say he's a profiteer, right enough, but he don't hire out the risky work."

Booger mulled that. "Mayhap you've struck a lode there. But you're takin' the long way around the barn, Trailsman. What you really wunner is if old Booger thinks he was hired to kill you?"

"Yeah—which of course means killing you, too."

"Of course," Booger repeated sarcastically. "Fargo, you are a filthy hyena! You share none o' the pussy with old Booger, but you'll push him right up front when the lead's a-flyin'! Anyhow, if this bastard Lomax has put a man on the coach, I'd bet my flap hat it's Ashton. Hell, them other two 'men' ain't naught but female boys."

"He seems most likely," Fargo agreed. "But I've learned the hard way that you can't always go by what seems most obvious. A killer needn't *look* like a killer."

"Well, there's the holy man. I cannot abide them perfumed whiskers! And that little piss squirt Malachi—all his gibberish about the Eighth House and moon pebbles could just be eyewash."

"I went through their pokes while they were asleep," Fargo admitted. "Unless they have hideout guns, neither man is heeled."

"Aye, and Ashton is. But does a pepperbox seem right for a hired killer? Why, it will ensure a kill at close range. But it fires all six loads at once, and once fired it's a hell-buster to reload—whichever one of us he *didn't* kill could burn him down before he even cleared the chambers."

"Yeah, I thought about that, too. Maybe he's got a hideout gun up his sleeve. Well . . . what about Trixie?"

Booger quickly turned his head to stare at Fargo. "Has your brain come unhinged? Send a woman to kill Skye Far—"

Booger suddenly caught himself. "Why, hell yes! Send a woman. They all get the tormentin' itch around Skye goldang Fargo, and that's all he expects of 'em. Why, if it's Trixie, old Booger's hat is off to her. The black-handed treachery of it brings tears to my eyes! Screw the very man you mean to kill just to put him off guard. Yessir, it's a capital hit and I admire it. But you don't truly suspect her, hey?"

"Tell you the truth, old son, I ain't got one shred of proof any of them passengers plan to kill me—us, I mean. So maybe we best worry about the cockroaches who *do* mean to plant us."

Fargo shifted his shell belt and resumed his close scrutiny of the surrounding terrain. During the next hour a Chinook brought in the rapid onset of dark, boiling thunderheads. Just north of the swing station at Alameda the heavens opened up with a vengeance, and a savage downpour reduced visibility to just a few feet. The rain tapered to a drizzle, but soon the coach began to lug from mud-caked wheels. Several times Fargo was forced to swing down and clear them.

On one of these occasions Kathleen poked her head outside. "Mr. Fargo? Do you think we'll reach Santa Fe on schedule?"

"I just can't say, lady. Booger tells me we're back on schedule now. But we're hitting the rough patch, and to tell you the truth, I expect hard sledding."

"Yes, that makes sense. I've never missed an opening date before."

"I know the show must go on and all that. But it's not just

a play that's in danger here. My job is to protect you, not some theater's profits."

She nodded. "I take your meaning, and I confess I'm frightened for myself. Especially since you're only being paid to assure my safe arrival in Santa Fe. What happens when you leave?"

Fargo knew the rest were listening. He lowered his voice. "It's not my way to leave a woman in the lurch. I got no idea how this deal is going to play out. With luck, Zack Lomax won't live to ever threaten you again. All I know is that I'm *not* going to quit this job—pay or no pay—until I know you're safe."

Her eyes suddenly filmed with tears, and only now did Fargo truly realize the fear and worry gnawing at her.

"Thank you . . . Skye. It's more loyalty than I deserve given my insults and high-handed treatment of you."

Fargo grinned. "I like a woman with spirit. Besides, I've enjoyed roweling you. You'll insult me again before we part, count on it."

Booger sent him a sly grin when Fargo had climbed topside. "You cunning son of a bitch, Fargo. I heard you whispering sweet nothings with Her Nibs. Still think you can trim her, uh?"

"Cat sits by the gopher hole," Fargo reminded him.

"Aye, until the yellow dogs run him off. Mr. Death is after us, catfish, coming with a bone in his teeth. We are the Grim Reaper's favorite boys now, and you sniffing about for quiff! Fargo, you are the world-beatingest son of a bitch I ever knew."

The Concord edged out of a long S-curve, and Fargo saw that the trail ahead dipped into a deep, sandy wash with steep, sloping, timbered sides.

"Rein in," he told Booger. "I don't like the look of this stretch."

"Haw, you four-legged oat burners!" Booger roared at the team, tightening the reins on the leaders and kicking the brake on.

"It's that ridge above us on the right," Fargo explained as he raised his field glasses. "Any shooters hiding up there have got a clear line of fire into that wash. The rain didn't get this far north, at least, so we won't be trapped in mud. But that sand will slow us."

Minutely he studied each section of the ridge, trying to decide which location he'd choose if he were an ambusher.

"There's nothing else for it," he finally decided. "Booger, get up a head of steam and shoot this coach through that wash—mister, I mean like grease through a goose. I got a God-fear about this one."

13

Only later, when it was too late, would Fargo realize his crucial mistake.

Concerned about that ridge, he paid scant attention to the trail itself.

"Everybody in the coach duck down!" he shouted at the passengers, his Henry already locked into his shoulder socket.

"Gerlong there!" Booger bellowed at the team, furiously lashing at the leaders. "G'long there! Whoop!"

The Concord hit the sandy wash at a two-twenty clip and immediately slowed in the sand. A moment later, Fargo was almost jarred off the box when the coach lurched hard to a stop.

Horses whickered in fright, Booger cursed, and when Fargo glanced to the front his stomach fisted in a knot: the team leaders were mired up to their shoulders in a pitfall trap!

"Roll off!" Fargo shouted to Booger even as a hammering racket of gunfire opened up from the ridge above the trail.

Just as Fargo hit the ground in a crouch a bullet whiffed in close enough to tug at his shirt. He scuttled around to the far side of the coach, where Booger had already flung open the door.

Several bullets had penetrated the Concord, and the passengers, pressed as low as they could, seemed frozen in place.

"*Out!*" Booger roared. "You're fish in a barrel!"

Ashton recovered first and tugged at Kathleen, who remained too petrified to move. Cursing them all for tangle-brained fools, Booger reached inside and plucked the actress out as if she were a mere sack of feathers, dropping her unceremoniously to the ground. He nabbed Trixie next. Ashton shoved the preacher and Malachi Feldman outside.

During this hurried evacuation the gunfire from above didn't let up, but Fargo noticed the shooters were deliberately avoiding the interior of the Concord.

"Keep down and stay close to the coach," Fargo ordered the passengers. "From their angle they can't hit you on this side, so just stay put."

The steady, sure resolve of his voice had a calming effect on the others. Fargo slithered under the coach and peered up the ridge. By now a haze of black-powder smoke marked the ambushers' position. At least two rifle muzzles spat orange spear tips of flame.

"They coulda killed all the horses by now," Booger said. "But they ain't hit one."

"They're under orders to let the coach get through on time," Fargo speculated. "It's me and you they're trying to kill. They want us to fire back so they can get a bead on us."

Fargo studied the slope leading up to the ridge. It was dotted with wild plum bushes and jack pine—not the best cover but adequate if he used it effectively.

"Booger, I'm gonna hook around and flank 'em. You set up diversionary fire, but for Christ sakes *don't* show yourself. I found out back at Bosque Grande that at least one of those bastards is a dead shot. Give them a fast initial burst to keep their heads down while I get to cover."

The gunfire from the ridge had tapered off as the attackers bided their time, waiting for targets—only two shooters, Fargo was convinced by now. He got into position behind the rear of the coach.

"Put at 'em!" he told Booger, and the moment the big-bore North & Savage started barking, Fargo sprang toward the slope, his Henry at a high port. He gained the safety of a plum bush without drawing fire and hoped that meant he hadn't been spotted.

Fargo knew he had to work fast if he wanted to retain the all-important element of surprise. Lomax's dirt-workers would soon twig the fact that only one man was firing back, and it wouldn't take long to suspect Fargo's play. Moving with the precision of a well-oiled machine, he leapfrogged from tree to bush, rapidly ascending the slope.

Taking advantage of an erosion seam, he crouched low

and gained the summit. Booger was still plinking from behind the coach, and Fargo realized the savvy former Indian fighter was shifting his position to mimic two shooters.

Fargo cautiously made his way along the exposed spine of the ridge, having spotted the ambush nest: a clutch of boulders about fifty yards ahead of him. At first he could see neither well-hidden man, just the boulders surrounded by a black haze of smoke. Then one of them ducked back behind the boulders and into Fargo's view.

Russ Alcott, reloading a long Jennings rifle. Fargo, bent low, started to shuck out his Colt, then decided against it. He was awkwardly straddling the ridge, and fifty yards was a tough shot with a six-gun even if a man was well balanced for steady aim. But before he could snap in for a shot with his Henry, Alcott spotted him.

Fargo's jaw slacked at the speed with which the hired gun dropped the rifle and filled both hands with blue steel. Two wooden-gripped Colt Navies opened up on him, and Fargo had no choice but to leap like a butt-shot dog, rolling sideways fast down the steep slope as bullets stitched the ground behind him in close pursuit. He barely managed to cover down behind a small boulder before the hot lead caught up to him.

"Fargo, you dug your own grave when you stuck your oar in my boat down in San Marcial!" the gunslick shouted. "I don't take guff from *no* crusading shit-heel like you! Won't be long, you'll be picking lead out of your liver!"

"That's mighty gaudy patter, Alcott!" Fargo called back. "The two-gun punks always like to hot-jaw. But Spider Winslowe ain't got much to say anymore, huh? Before too long you're gonna be mighty quiet, too."

Another burst of lead peppered the small boulder and forced Fargo to make love to the ground. Whatever else Alcott was, he was some pumpkins with a handgun—very few men could score hits, at this range and angle, with anything less than a rifle. Fargo knew that he couldn't expose himself to return fire against this remarkable shootist—not if he wanted to see another sunrise.

Thirty seconds of silence were followed by the rataplan of shod hooves escaping down the back of the ridge. By the time Fargo gained the spine again, the two horsebackers were rapidly retreating through a grassy draw. Fargo only had time to get off a ranging shot before a motte of pine swallowed them.

He fought down a welling of angry frustration. "Well, *that* was a slick operation," he informed the landscape, his tone laced with disgust aimed at himself.

"Fargo!" Booger's voice thundered from the trail below. "Do I finally get to piss on your grave?"

"Not today, you ugly mange-pot!"

Fargo retreated down the slope to join the others. Booger had already blindfolded the team leaders to calm them so he could free them from the twisted harness.

"Sounded like they got away," Ashton greeted him.

Fargo nodded. "My fault. I let Alcott get the drop on me."

"Maybe you scared them off for good this time," Kathleen suggested, her tone hopeful.

Fargo shook his head. "Don't seem likely. These two are hard cases on the prod. They know they'll be boosted branchward if the law ever catches them, so they've got nothing to lose by racking up a few more kills—and Zack Lomax's money to gain if they prevail. Either we take the bull by the horns or we get gored."

He glanced toward Booger. "Are the horses all right?"

"Aye, once we calm 'em down."

"You three men," Fargo said, "get a wiggle on. Give Booger a hand wrangling the horses out. Ladies, back in the coach. I'm gonna tack my horse and ride back up that ridge."

"But why?" Trixie said. "You said they're gone."

"To stand guard until we move out. Those two killers could be doubling back right now to jump us again before we clear this wash. And this time I don't plan to be afoot. I've had my belly full of these hit-and-run ambushes. My stallion can outrun his own shadow, and if I spot those two egg-sucking varmints while I'm horsed, they won't get another chance to show yellow."

Fargo didn't get his chance to take the bull by the horns.

As the sun flamed out in the west, the trapped leaders were freed and hitched into the traces without incident.

Fargo, disappointed that the two attackers hadn't returned, rode down from the ridge.

"How long you figure before we reach San Felipe?" Fargo asked Booger as he prepared to lash the team into motion.

"Three hours if it's smooth sailing."

"We best not light the running lamps," Fargo said. "Both those rat bastards can hold and squeeze. I'll be riding spotter just ahead of the coach in case there's any problems with the trail."

"There's only two of them sons-a-bitches," Booger scoffed. "Us two mighty bastards whipped ten times that many Comanches at Antelope Wells."

"We did, and a good day's work at that. But we were forted up and they attacked us across open ground. Still, I can't see these two attacking after dark if the running lamps are out. It's clear now they don't wanna kill Kathleen, just nab her. If they open up on us in the dark, they risk hitting her."

The coach was in motion now, Fargo riding alongside while some daylight remained. Booger hooked a thumb over his shoulder and lowered his voice.

"Only a couple days left now, catfish. Might be trouble real close to home, if you take my drift?"

Fargo nodded. Despite watching all the passengers closely since leaving El Paso, he had no proof one of them worked for Lomax. But Lansford Ashton, especially, worried him—the "businessman's agent" exuded a cool confidence and impressive intellect, and his reticence about himself suggested a man who harbored secrets.

"Mr. McTeague," Kathleen called out, "are you certain there are bathing facilities at San Felipe?"

Booger grinned and winked at Fargo. "As sure as God made little green apples, Your Loveliness," Booger assured her. "You'll have a nice hot bath. San Felipe is one of the finest stations on the line."

"Yes, you said that about that . . . that roach hole at Los Pinos."

"Aye, old Booger played high jinks there, lass. But though a dog may return to his own vomit, Booger don't. You'll have a relaxing bath and a hot meal."

Booger snickered, but when Fargo looked a question at

him, the shaggy giant merely played the innocent. "Gerlong there!" he barked at the leaders, snapping his six-horse whip.

When night had drawn her sable curtain, Fargo gigged the Ovaro out in front, staying about fifty yards ahead of the coach. He knew that another pitfall would be nearly impossible to spot at night, but he had to take the risk. The Ovaro occasionally chafed at the sedate pace and fought the bit, but was also clearly content to be under the saddle again rather than being towed like a milk cow.

Around ten p.m. they reached the station house at San Felipe, and Kathleen Barton's mood underwent a sea change. Booger had told the truth: the place was clean and comfortable, by way-station standards, and the Mexican station master showed the relieved actress a ladies' bathhouse featuring a long steel tub rather than the usual round wooden model made by sawing a whiskey barrel in half.

While water was being heated for bathing, the station master's wife served a palatable meal of roast chicken, potatoes, and greens. Booger, Fargo noticed, seemed especially excited and sent Fargo several conspiratorial winks.

"What's that you got there?" Fargo asked Trixie while the travelers enjoyed hot coffee, sweetened with Gail Borden's new canned milk, after their meal.

"Oh, it's just something I clipped out of *Harper's* a few years back," she replied. "A little verse by Sarah Bolton. I liked it so much I glued it on this piece of pasteboard. Now and then I look at it—it's sorter a, whatchacallit, a philosophy I try to live by."

She handed Fargo the clipping and he read it aloud:

> Voyage upon life's sea,
> To yourself be true,
> And whatever your lot may be,
> Paddle your own canoe.

Trixie blushed. "It's silly, I s'pose."

"Paddle your own canoe, huh?" Fargo repeated. "I like that just fine."

Booger, who had generously laced his coffee with whiskey, was in his usual belligerent mood. "Paddle a cat's tail!

Fargo, your wick is flickering. That's sweet-lavender claptrap. Can you eat it, drink it, or fuc—ahh, diddle it? If not, throw it away."

"Vulgar nonsense, Mr. McTeague," Kathleen put in. "It's good advice for a young woman to follow."

"Magazine claptrap," Booger insisted. "Writers are the maggots of society. Lookit how them quill merchants color Fargo up: 'a true knight in buckskins.' Pah! Why, *look* at his pretty teeth! The vain little nancy is alla time workin' 'em with a hog-bristle brush to impress the calicos."

"Maybe so," Fargo replied good-naturedly, "but at least I don't have to gum my food like you do."

"If you knew how to read, Mr. McTeague," the preacher chimed in, "you'd realize all you've been missing in the Scriptures, the divine inspiration of an All-wise Providence. You mock your God, sir, but 'whatsoever a man soweth, that shall he also reap.' Prepare for the cold, inevitable grave and the hellfire to follow—repent!"

Booger banged his cup down and brandished a fist. "So you, too, have tired of eating solid food, eh? Preacher, Booger McTeague is a ravenous, man-eating son of a bitch, savvy that? I will shoot you in the face and laugh while you die! I—"

"Senorita," the station master's wife called to Kathleen, "your bath is ready."

Booger instantly forgot his tirade, grinned slyly, and caught the Trailsman's eye. "Fargo," he said almost meekly, "step outside, won't you? I'd like a bit of chin-wag with you."

"The hell's this all about?" Fargo demanded when they were out in the yard.

"Did not old Booger promise you a surprise? Follow me."

Booger led the way around to the back of the station house. Moonlight revealed a plank door at the rear.

"Supply room," he explained, fishing a key from his hip pocket. "Only the station master is allowed in and out, but I bribed Hernando for the spare key."

Booger unlocked the door and grabbed the coal-oil lantern hanging on a nail beside it. He scratched a phosphor to life and turned up the wick, lighting it. Then he led Fargo into a small room crowded with crates, sacks of grain, harness gear and other supplies.

Fargo said, "What are—"

"Shush it!" Booger whispered. "Keep your voice low, Trailsman. That wall ahead of us is made from cheap flock-board. C'mon."

Booger's excitement was palpable. They crossed the room and drew up in front of a calendar advertising the New Haven Arms factory. Booger snuffed the lantern and plucked the calendar off the wall. Two perfectly round peepholes had been drilled through the wall about a foot apart. Light beamed through them.

Booger leaned close to Fargo's ear. "That's the ladies bathhouse on the other side," he said in a gloating whisper. "And I drilled these on a plumb line with the tub. I *told* you we'd see her naked."

"Now, hold on here," Fargo whispered back. "This is low even for you."

"Low is it? Then clear on out, knight in buckskins, for *this* horny knave means to see America's Sweetheart in the raw. G'long, Fargo—p'r'aps that yapping preacher has got you pious."

"Well . . . hell, long as I'm already here . . ."

Both men pressed an eye to the peepholes. Fargo instantly spotted Kathleen, flatteringly illuminated in the light of a six-branch candelabra. She had just taken down her thick, coffee-colored hair, and now it tumbled over her shoulders and framed that perfect face.

The station master's wife must have helped Kathleen, before she left, with the stays of her velvet traveling dress, for now she shrugged easily out of it and folded it on a chair. Her slim silk chemise showed two dark dimples where her nipples dented the sheer fabric. She slid it over her head, and Fargo suddenly felt his heartbeat throbbing hard in his palms at the sight of her bare tits.

Booger sucked in a hissing breath, then excitedly poked Fargo hard with his elbow. "Oh, Jerusalem! Her jahoobies ain't quite as big as Trixie's," he whispered, "but she ain't no member of the itty-bitty-titty club, neither. There's *way* more than a mouthful there, catfish."

Fargo admired form more than size, and Kathleen's breasts, like her face, could have been sculpted by Michelangelo.

The pert, strawberry nipples were surrounded by aureoles the color of sunlit honey.

She laid the chemise atop her dress, then pulled off her knee-length, ruffled pantalets and stepped out of them, leaving them in a puddle on the floor. Now she stood completely naked, and Fargo almost forgot to breathe.

Kathleen was not as buxom as Trixie, nor did she have her flaring hourglass hips. But the beautifully tapering thighs and calves, the gently curving stomach and perfect breasts, the exciting "V" of silky mons hair, the gorgeous face and flawless opal skin painted a picture of female perfection unsurpassed in Fargo's vast experience. "Greek goddess" were the words that immediately came to mind.

"Jesus K. T. Christ," Booger whispered. "She ain't no stable filly," was all he could muster—in Fargo's mind perhaps the century's greatest understatement.

The long steel tub projected from the wall opposite them in perfect line with the peepholes, offering both voyeurs a full view of the beautiful actress when she had stretched out in the soothing bath. But neither man expected what began to happen next.

Kathleen slid both hands up to her breasts and took both nipples between thumb and forefinger. Slowly, at first, and then gradually more rapidly she rolled them until they were so hard and swollen they looked like little strawberry thumbs.

"Jumpin' Jupiter!" Booger emitted a little moan of excitement and Fargo elbowed him quiet.

One hand continued to stimulate her nipples while the other glided down to her stomach and then inched through the silky delta of mons hair. She bent her legs up and spread her creamy thighs wider, and now both men had a clear shot of the lovely coral grotto as her fingers probed lower.

Fargo felt the throbbing weight of his arousal as his manhood ploughed a hard furrow down one leg of his buckskins. By now Booger was barely able to contain himself. The man-mountain almost knocked Fargo over when he elbowed him. "God's trousers, Skye! She's . . . why, she's diddlin' herself!"

"Damn it," Fargo whispered back, rubbing his sore ribs,

"keep your voice down, mooncalf. And stop leaning into that wall so hard—I can feel it bending."

Fargo forgot all else, however, when this vision of erotic loveliness began rubbing the chamois-soft hood over her sensitive pearl, her head starting to roll back and forth, her breathing growing deeper and faster, her face flushed as she pleasured herself toward higher and higher peaks. Her fingers soon moved so fast in the water that they made sounds like a hungry kitten lapping milk. Her lips began to form words in a hoarse whisper.

"Oh . . . yes . . . I'm . . . I'm close . . . oh, *yes*, Skye, I'm going to ex*plode*!" she moaned, and she did just that, jack-knifing almost double and crying out sharply as the mother of all climaxes racked her entire body and sloshed water onto the floor.

Hearing Fargo's name startled Booger, who was already pressing dangerously hard into the weak flock-board. Abruptly the wall collapsed and Booger crashed through it, doing a desperate Virginia reel to keep his balance. But disaster heaped on disaster when he tripped and smashed onto one corner of the tub, spilling the water and a shocked Kathleen onto the floor.

The actress was too astonished to even scream. For the first time in his life, Fargo saw Booger blush. He scrambled to his feet, averting his eyes and trying to stammer an apology. But the man whose tongue usually outpaced his brain now reminded Fargo of a snake trying to get started on loose sand.

"Why . . . that is to say . . . you see, I . . . Miss Barton, it was Fargo talked me into this black deed!"

Booger, his clothes sopping, fled out the door. Fargo should have fled by now also, but still he stood gazing through the ruined wall, unable to take his eyes off the naked woman sprawled on the floor. She met his eyes.

"I would expect a schoolboy trick like this from that big bumpkin," she told him. "But I'm surprised *you* would resort to illicit spying on a woman's bath, Mr. Fargo. You're hardly what I would call woman starved."

She caught sight of the impressive swelling in his buck-skin trousers and pried her eyes away only with obvious difficulty. "I see that the view pleases you. I suppose the two of you will now make a whore of me with your talk?"

"You suppose wrong. Take my word for it, me and Booger both know we were in the wrong. He didn't blush like that because he thinks you're a whore."

"I appreciate that much, at least. But don't you think it's time you put an end to this brazen effrontery and leave me to what's left of my privacy, Mr. Fargo?"

Fargo swallowed hard to regain his voice. But her haughty, dismissive tone convinced him that she needed to be taught a little lesson. The faint shadow of a smile touched his lips.

"Why not call me Skye . . . Kathleen? After all, you did just a minute ago."

"You mean you . . .?" Words failed her as she realized he'd heard the name she cried out in her flight of passion. Mortification seized her, then defensive anger to cover her shame. "Why, you arrogant, insufferable, immoral . . ."

Fargo ducked when she suddenly sat up and threw a hard lump of soap at him. He tossed back his head and laughed. "All right, I'm going, Princess. But I'm gonna have you on my mind, girl. Oh, am I gonna have you on my mind."

14

San Felipe station, in Fargo's estimation, lay dangerously close to Santa Fe—especially considering that the fatal deadline of June nineteenth was only two days off, and Zack Lomax had to be desperate by now to seize the reins before his master plan careened out of control. So Fargo and Booger went turnabout on sentry duty, dividing the remainder of the night.

Fargo stood the second stint from two a.m. until sunrise. He patrolled the big yard, the corral, and the stock barn in a random pattern taking advantage of a moon bright enough to make shadows. He circled the station house frequently, pausing often to listen to the night.

Eventually the monotony took its toll on his hair-trigger alertness. Fargo had slept little since this dangerous mission began eight days ago in El Paso, and cobwebs of exhaustion clung to his senses. And every time he rounded the back corner of the station where the women slept, images of a naked Kathleen Barton further derailed his vigilance.

During this long stint of guard duty, Fargo occasionally heard the mournful howl of a coyote, and each time he thought of the Apaches. It didn't seem likely the decimated band under Red Sash would be raiding again this soon, but other bands had been terrorizing the Christianized pueblos in the nearby mountain ranges.

Now and then, when sleep fumes began to cloud his thinking, Fargo stopped at the pump and doused his head in cool water. The night dragged on, the moon slowly fading from yellow to pale white, the polestar to the north gradually losing its shimmer before fading completely. One by one the constellations, which Fargo had learned long ago to identify and orient to, winked out.

Finally the soft glow known as false dawn—herald of the real thing—illumined the indigo sky to the east. Fargo was making his latest circle around the station house when the Ovaro suddenly gave his trouble whicker.

It brought Fargo fully alert like a slap to the face. He pressed flat against a front corner of the house, levering the Henry and holding it against his chest. His eyes, fully adjusted for night vision, quickly scanned the area. The stock barn loomed beyond the corral, a shadowy silhouette against the sky.

Maybe, he reasoned, it was just the *mozo* or a stock-tender stirring around that had alerted the Ovaro. But Fargo had not survived this long by assuming the best. He resumed his careful study.

Besides the station house and the barn there were two small outbuildings, one a shack where soap was made, the other an outdoor privy. What was it about the privy, he wondered, that seemed different from the last time he'd glanced at it?

The door, his mind answered. It was open before, but now it's closed.

Fargo knew someone could have used it during the night, but could he have been unaware of the visit? True, his vigilance had waned at times, but not that much.

He grounded his Henry and shucked out his Colt, crossing the yard at an oblique angle toward that door. The closer he got to it the louder his pulse throbbed in his ears—closed and half-open doors had come to symbolize, for Fargo, the unknown terror that could shape a man's destiny. They sometimes divided two worlds—life and death—and flinging the wrong door open could plunge a man into the "eternal movelessness" of death that lurked just beyond a thin slab of wood.

Stopping fifteen feet back and off to one side, he called out, "Come on out, whoever you are, or I'll turn that crapper into a sieve!"

Only the soft soughing of a cool night breeze answered his challenge.

"The fox play didn't work," Fargo called out. "Now show yourself before I blast you to chair stuffings!"

Again nothing but a soft, moaning breeze that seemed to mock his suspicion. Doubt assailed Fargo. Maybe a snake had set the Ovaro off, and certainly the breeze could have nudged that door shut. Was he really going to open up on a probably empty shithouse and scare hell out of everyone at the station?

He started toward the door, feeling foolish. But just then the fine hairs on his nape prickled. *The readiness is all, Fargo!*

He turned sideways to reduce his target profile and edged closer, standing to one side and wedging the muzzle of his Colt between the rickety, weather-beaten door and its frame.

The door creaked slowly open with a sound like a rusty nail being pulled out. Nothing. Almost convinced by now the outhouse was empty Fargo nonetheless erred on the side of caution. He pulled his Colt back, hung his hat on it, and eased it inside.

The sudden, unexpected sound of a six-gun erupting was obscenely loud and iced Fargo's blood. His gun was knocked from his hand and clattered to the plank floor of the privy. Quicker than a blink the hidden man leaped outside and crouched, pivoting toward Fargo.

All this was quick as a rattlesnake striking. Over the years Fargo had honed a special knack for separating himself from a crisis moment, for becoming both participant and observer at the same time. Fargo the participant wanted to reflexively dive to safety while going for the Arkansas toothpick in his boot sheath; Fargo the observer, however, warned him there wasn't time—weapons would not save his life this time.

Fargo resorted to his long, strong legs, kicking up savagely and connecting with the six-shooter just as the gunman fired. The Trailsman felt a razor-burn of pain as the diverted bullet grazed his right cheek. Fargo waded in fast and threw a powerful haymaker that rocked the man's head backward, his teeth clacking like dice. Fargo followed up with a vicious uppercut. The assailant's knees bellied and he flopped face-first into the ground, unconscious.

"H'ar now!" Booger's voice bellowed from in front of the house. "Fargo, you better be dead! My dream was about to turn wet when this infernal racket rousted me!"

"Sorry to spoil your big time," Fargo called back. "Booger, bring that lantern over here."

Fargo rolled the intruder over and extracted the Remington from his hand, then searched him. He found an ivory-grip over-and-under hideout pistol in the inside pocket of his rawhide vest.

"What's this?" Booger demanded as he arrived with the lantern. "Did this shithouse rat bite you?"

The groaning man regained consciousness, blood flowing copiously from his broken lips and teeth. Fargo took in the flat, mud-colored eyes and the tight-to-the-bone skin of his face.

"Recognize him?" Fargo asked Booger, handing him the weapons.

"I recolleck that ugly dial from somewheres. He 'minds me of a face I seen on a wanted dodger in El Paso. Shall I lop off his nuts?"

"You two got it all wrong," the man said through swelling lips. "I was just takin' a dump when this bearded hombre commenced to threatening my life. I only fired in self-defense."

Fargo slapped him repeatedly and hard. "Bottle it, numb-nuts. Who gave you your marching orders to kill me?"

Fargo's face etched itself in stone in the yellow lantern light. Again he repeatedly slapped the man, rocking his head fast from side to side. "How much did Lomax pay you to kill me, puke pail?"

"Mister, you must be moonstruck! I ain't no hired killer, and I don't know this Lomax. My name is Ansel Munro. I'm on my way to Santa Fe to find work in the silver mines."

"Sure," Fargo said, "and I'm the Romish Pope. You're just a miner with a tied-down holster and a hideout gun. This time of night you can take a shit anywhere without trespassing on posted land. And I gave you a call-out—all you had to do was speak up and step outside, but you tried to murder me. Now I'm asking you again—who paid you to kill me?"

"Skye?" Trixie's worried voice called out. "What's going on?"

The day was on the brink of sunrise and Fargo could make out several people in the yard near the house.

"You folks go on inside," he told them. "Me and Booger will handle this."

Fargo still knelt on one knee beside the supine man. "Talk out, damn you, or you'll wish you'd died as a child. You murdering pig's afterbirth, *who* hired you?"

"Go piss up a rope, cockchafer. I'm done talking."

"Ha-ho, ha-ho!" Booger exclaimed. "So this one's about half rough, is he? Fargo, I know you're squeamish, so give old Booger your toothpick and I'll lop off his nuts. The sac will make a fine tobacco pouch once it's cured."

"I see no reason to coddle him like that," Fargo replied. "Ask Hernando for a shovel. We're gonna dig a honey hole for this scum bucket."

"*That's* the ticket!" Booger said gleefully. "Fargo, you are a diabolical son of a bitch and I wish to have your child. Yes, a honey hole! By the Lord Harry he *will* talk, hey?"

By the time the new day's sun was giving its first warmth, the man who called himself Ansel Munro was buried up to his neck behind the station house.

"Mister, this ain't no way to treat a white man," the would-be murderer protested.

"Aye," Booger agreed heartily. "We shoulda shot you in the whang first. But the best is yet to come, boyo. Great larks ahead!"

By now the rest were too curious to wait in the house. Ignoring Fargo's order, they had assembled in the yard nearby.

"Hernando," Fargo said, "you got any honey or molasses?"

"A big can of molasses, Senor Fargo."

"Good. Fetch it out here, wouldja?"

"The hell?" the buried man protested. "Mister, what're you doing?"

"See those mounds about four feet away? Those are anthills—red ants. The meanest kind. I'm gonna smear this molasses all over your head. Once those ants pick up the smell, they'll swarm your head by the thousands. And they won't stop eating until they're down to the skull."

"Oh, it's a screechin' misery," Booger chimed in, rubbing his hands together briskly. "Takes hours for them little mites to sup full. The eyeballs will go first, and they'll stream up your nostrils—"

"Gentlemen," the preacher cut in, "this is not Christian."

"Shut your cake-hole, nervous Nellie," Booger snapped.

"Skye, are'n'cha taking this a little too far?" Trixie asked.

"I *could* just send him to glory with a clean head shot," Fargo conceded. "We're under territorial law and he signed his own death warrant when he made an attempt on my life. But, see, the man who hired him doesn't want to be put over the fence into the open. I mean to prove, once and for all in front of witnesses, it was Zack Lomax."

Hernando returned with a big can of molasses. The killer's face turned pale as alkali dust.

"His name ain't Lomax," he finally gave in. "It's Cort Bergman. He lives in Santa Fe."

"Describe him," Fargo demanded.

"Middling height, plenty of muscles, wears his hair in one a them high whatchacallits."

"Pompadour?"

"Yeah. But it's his eyes that you first notice—they sorter bore into a man, like, and force you to look away."

Kathleen gasped. "It's Lomax! He *is* still alive!"

"All right," Fargo said. "Everybody here is a witness—this jasper admits Lomax hired him to kill me."

"Mr. Fargo," Kathleen said, "what are you going to do with this man? Surely you can't just leave him here?"

Fargo had already pondered that dilemma. Despite having the legal right to kill him, Fargo was not comfortable with summary execution. Every man he had ever killed had an even chance.

But it was Hernando who resolved the situation.

"Senorita Barton," he said, "it is out of Fargo's hands. As station master *I* am the authority on this Overland property. This man attempted to kill an employee of Overland, and with no other law the matter is up to me. Nothing will happen while you two ladies are here. And there will be no use of ants or molasses. Now, *por favor*, put it from your mind."

Booger stared at the preacher. "Like you was spoutin' to me last night: As ye reap, so shall ye sew. You got a complaint, psalm singer?"

"The Old Testament is very much a part of the Good Book, Mr. McTeague. It was the business with the red ants I deplored. Now we must render unto Caesar those things which *are* Caesar's."

"Great day in the morning!" Booger exclaimed. "The Rev's got a pair on him after all!"

After a hot breakfast of eggs and the spiced sausage called chorizo, the Santa Fe–bound travelers again headed north. Fargo was astride the Ovaro now, riding close to the Concord. Perhaps five minutes after the coach rolled out, a lone gunshot echoed from the San Felipe station.

"Well, catfish," Booger remarked, "at least we done most of the burying for Hernando."

Fargo nodded. "Yeah, and now we've confirmed it's Lomax behind all the trouble. But the sick son of a bitch is getting desperate. Booger, these next two days will be a hell buster."

Fargo's grim prediction started coming true even sooner than he expected.

The first swing station after San Felipe was La Cruz, about a three-hour drive. But the agitated swingman greeted them with bad news: snipers, hidden in a nearby tree line, had killed all of the fresh relay horses in less than a minute of withering fire.

"W'an a damn thing I could do, Booger," the aging employee explained. "It all happened quicker 'n scat. A dozen horses dropped, and when I tried to let a few of the rest escape the pole corral, one of them-air shooters blowed my conk cover off. Hell, I had to kiss the dirt or they'da bucked *me* out."

"Bad medicine," Booger told Fargo. "These teams are working harder now to pull up some long, steep slopes, and mayhap we'll get stranded agin like we done after Los Pinos."

"My guess," Fargo said, "is that Alcott and his partner ain't worried about the schedule now. We saw the mirror-relay—likely they've got new orders to snatch Kathleen and get her to Lomax by the nineteenth—tomorrow sometime. Which still means they have to kill me and you, and that's easier to do if they strand us."

Booger tilted his head toward the nearby coach. "Happens that's so, Trailsman, why'n't we take Ashton's pepper-box from him. *He* could be getting desperate, too."

Fargo grinned. "Don't fret that crowd leveler of his—it ain't worth an old underwear button now. The firing pin is in my pocket. I took it out while he was asleep. He likely has a hideout gun, too, but he'll try to use the big gun first, so we'll be warned. When's the next swing station?"

"Diablo. It'd be 'bout two and a half hours with a fresh team. With stale horses, we won't likely get there until the middle of the afternoon."

"Could be a lively ride, too. And who's to say the horses won't be slaughtered there, too?"

Booger loosed a streamer. "Happens *that's* so, catfish, we'll all be rowed up Salt Creek. The next full station is Domingo, but we got switchbacks and hills, and this team won't hold up even with our two extras. It'll be shank's mare or a night camp."

They pulled out, Fargo riding ahead of the swift wagon but never losing sight of it, hoping to draw any ambush fire onto himself. He read the wildly varying terrain with the eye of a veteran scout: low red and purple mesas, scattered tumbles of boulders, slopes covered with dull, dusty chaparral. He also kept a wary eye on the trail, looking for any signs of another pitfall trap.

The day heated up until, by noon, a furnace-hot sun blazed straight overhead. By now the worn-out team was dragging in the traces, and Booger had cursed himself hoarse prodding them. His whip cracked constantly now, and on the steeper grades he ordered the three men out to walk alongside, lightening the load.

When it was almost two by the sun, Booger stopped to breathe the horses and Fargo reined around to join the others. Kathleen Barton, obviously mortified at what Booger and Fargo had seen and heard the night before, purposely avoided his eyes.

Booger handed his flask to Fargo, who took a small jolt to cut the dust.

"Faugh!" Booger mocked him. "Skye, how many times must I instruct you? When it comes to drinkin' whiskey, it's better to go down hard than to hedge."

"When I'm under the gun I stay sober. Might be a good idea for you, too."

Booger winked at Fargo and hooked a thumb down toward the passengers. He deliberately raised his voice so Kathleen would hear. "Oh, Skye, if I don't get my proper ration I will ex*plode*!"

"Oh, that's very humorous, Mr. McTeague," she retorted, acid dripping from her words.

"Booger," Trixie called out, "can I ride up on the high seat? It's hot as the hinges of Hades back here."

"Too dangerous," Fargo told her.

Kathleen finally met Fargo's eyes. "I see. You worry about women's safety, but not at all about their privacy or feminine dignity?"

"I know I'm in your bad books, Miss Barton," he replied, "and I went too far last night. But I'd be a damn hypocrite if I told you I regret it. No harm was done, so why don't we just sign a peace treaty?"

After a moment her expressive lips formed the beginning of a smile. "Yes, why don't we? It hardly makes sense to be at daggers drawn with my bodyguard."

"What happened last night?" Trixie asked, curious.

Fargo saw all three of the men staring expectantly at Kathleen.

"Nothing she was responsible for," he replied curtly. "Booger, you ready to roll this rig?"

They finally reached the Diablo swing station just after three p.m. and Fargo, riding vanguard, saw in an instant that they were now truly up against it. He hauled back on the Ovaro's reins and threw a leg over the cantle, dismounting. He tossed the reins forward to hold his stallion, who whiffed the powerful blood smell and gave a nervous whicker.

Dead horses dotted the corral. As the stagecoach rolled up

behind him, Fargo crossed the corral toward a despondent-looking man with big pouches like bruises under his eyes. Blood stained the right arm of his shirt. Booger hustled to catch up with Fargo.

"You hit bad, Jed?" Booger greeted the dazed swingman.

"Nah, just nicked me. Damn it all, Booger! I never even spotted the shooters. I was pouring grain into the trough, and all of a sudden-like, lead was flyin' ever which-way."

Fargo looked at Booger. "What about the station at Domingo? Can they kill the relays there, too?"

"Don't seem likely. There's six Overland workers there, all armed. 'Sides, the teams will be in a stock barn, not an open corral like this. But Christ Almighty, Fargo, this team is blown in. The hell we do now—sit and play a harp?"

"I been studying on that," Jed said. "You heard of Harley Doyle?"

Booger said, "You mean the mustanger who catches scrubs and breaks 'em to leather?"

Jed nodded. "It's a long shot, but he's got him a spread close by and he might have some horses could maybe be harnessed."

"Combination horses?" Booger asked, meaning horses broken to saddle and harness.

"Seems to me he only breaks 'em to the saddle. He don't geld his stallions, neither, and them bastards won't harness without raisin' one helluva ruckus—you'd want mares. Most of his stock are just Indian scrubs, fourteen, fifteen hands high. But now and then he gets some Arabians in his catch pens."

Booger pulled on his chin, mulling it. "Trouble is we can't use our two spare bays as leaders—scrub mares won't likely pull behind geldings. We'd hafta use at least two stallions as leaders."

Booger looked at Fargo. "We'd play hell getting scrubs harnessed to that swift wagon. But it beats just lollygaggin' around here."

Fargo nodded. "Where can I find Doyle?" he asked the swingman.

Jed pointed west. "See that tree with its top sliced off by lightning? Doyle's place is just a half mile past it."

"You boys unhitch this team," Fargo said as he started toward the Ovaro. "And, Booger, keep a close eye on Kathleen."

Fargo found Doyle walking a mustang in circles around a breaking pole. He quickly explained the urgent situation and assured Doyle that Overland would pay the going rate for six horses.

"Hell, it ain't the money, Mr. Fargo," Doyle assured him. "When folks're in a bind, it's a man's Christian duty to help out. And I got the horses—strong barbs," he added, meaning Arabians. "I just ain't a-tall sure it can be did. See, my insides is all shot to hell from my bronc-bustin' days. That means that I can only sorter gentle them scrubs some—you know, get 'em use to the man smell and to the feel of a saddle. I sell 'em cheap at the Santa Fe horse auctions as half-broke. Whoever buys 'em has to actually break these scrubs to a rider."

Doyle glanced uncertainly toward the corral. "As to puttin' 'em in harness—might be easier to stick a wolverine down your pants."

"But it could possibly be done?"

"Well, with blindfolds we can move them to the swing station and likely get them scrubs into the traces. But once we jerk them blinds off? Mister, them sons-a-bucks will commence to running full tilt, and I do mean *tilt*—they might leave the trail and turn your rig over at a damn high speed. It would take one helluva driver to control them."

"We've got one helluva driver—Booger McTeague."

"Booger! Hell, that's different. *He* might be able to control 'em. I see you got one more advantage—that fine-looking stallion you ride. Run him right out front as the master stallion and the rest just *might* follow him."

Doyle, limping noticeably, led Fargo toward a big pole corral. "Mr. Fargo, I oughter warn you—even if Booger can avoid a rollover, once these scrubs commence to a panic run they *won't* stop."

"Would a wire bit cutting into their mouths," Fargo asked, "haul them in?"

"Nope, I've tried that. I've watched wild horses run all day, and I guarantee they'll still be running hard when you hit Domingo—they won't stop until their hearts give out. I hope that stallion of yours is as smart as he looks because he's the best chance you got."

15

Doyle picked out six of his strongest, biggest horses and tied blindfolds on them. Then, to control them for the brief ride back to the swing station, he "necked" them in pairs to a single lead line. Even with these precautions the half-wild stock gave Doyle and Fargo fits trying to control them—and Fargo misgivings about this harebrained plan.

Rollovers were common even with well-trained Cleveland bays, and Fargo knew that sometimes these accidents seriously injured or even killed passengers. And at the breakneck pace Doyle swore these scrubs would maintain, a rollover could prove disastrous.

But Fargo saw no better way out of this fix, and it was imperative to get Kathleen and the rest of these passengers to Domingo. If any driver could pull this off, it was Booger McTeague.

While Booger and Doyle fought to harness the blind-folded horses, Fargo spoke to the passengers.

"Folks, we're trapped between a rock and a hard place. This is going to be a fast, hard ride and you've *got* to cooperate for your own safety. Booger can't ride the brake at a fast pace. The thoroughbraces on this Concord will help, but it's going to toss you around like rubber balls if you don't do as I tell you."

Fargo flung one of the doors open. "I want that middle seat left empty so you can use it to brace yourselves. Ashton, you're the strongest, so I want you right next to Kathleen in her usual seat at the rear. I want Trixie in the middle of the front seat with Malachi and the preacher on either side of her. You men, it's up to you to keep the women secure in their seats. Hold them down, damn it, no matter what. If the coach rolls—"

"Rolls?" Malachi paled. "Why, we'll all be—"

"Just nerve up and listen to me. *If* the coach rolls, don't anybody get any foolish notions about leaping out. Nine times out of ten your best chance is to stay in the rig. It's damn well constructed, and you can see the thick leather padding."

"Skye, Booger said it's only about twelve miles to Domingo," Trixie said. "Maybe we should just walk."

Fargo shook his head. "We'd be picked off like lice on a blanket. Same problem if we just stay here and wait for the next stagecoach. There's only two runs a week on this line, and that next stage is three days behind us."

"I string along with Fargo," Ashton said. "I was in a roll-over once outside San Bernardino. A few of us got bruised up, and one fellow got his nose broken, but we all survived."

"Yes," Malachi said, "but how fast were you going?"

"Not very," Ashton admitted. "The driver was drunk and we went over on a soft shoulder."

"Booger is a good driver," Trixie said.

"But usually drunk," the preacher added.

"Never mind," Fargo snapped. "We ain't putting this to a vote. The team's almost ready. You folks take your seats like I told you and brace as best you can on that middle seat. You men, it's up to you to protect those women."

"Will *you* be on the coach?" Pastor Brandenburg said spitefully. "Taking the risk with the rest of us?"

"I'll be where I'm most useful, Rev. Now chuck the flap-jaw and get in that coach."

By now it was late afternoon with perhaps three hours of daylight left. Booger climbed up on the box, pulled on his gauntlets, and seized his whip. "Let her rip!" he shouted.

Fargo, Harley Doyle and Jed the swingman had each lined up: Doyle with the leaders, Jed the swing team, Fargo the wheel team. At Booger's command they pulled off the blindfolds and the six terrified, mostly wild horses surged forward.

Fargo vaulted into his saddle and gigged the Ovaro out in front of the leaders. In no time at all, the relay scrubs were running full bore, defying all efforts by Booger to slow them down. Fargo was forced to open the Ovaro out to a lope to stay ahead.

At first the stage road was level, smooth and fairly straight, and dust billowed behind as the coach made excellent time. Fargo, his Henry resting behind the pommel, kept a close eye on both sides, watching for an ambush. Booger's whip continued to crack, but not to spur on the team—that would have been like pouring kerosene on flames given their headlong, breakneck pace. Rather, his constant effort was aimed at keeping them on the road, for the uneven, rocky terrain on both sides would quickly cause a dangerous rollover.

Fargo and the Ovaro assisted his efforts. Each time the swift wagon wandered too close to unstable terrain, Fargo dropped back and hazed the leaders back on course. At times the road turned washboard, and only Booger's formidable size and weight kept him on the box when the Concord bounced and rocked recklessly. Now and again all four wheels left the road, and only its superior, nearly indestructible construction kept it intact each time it crashed back down.

Above the thundering racket of hooves, slamming wheels and Booger's booming curses, Fargo could hear Malachi Feldman bawling like a bay steer.

"Stop! Oh, land love us, please *stop*! We'll be dashed to—*ouch!*—pieces!"

Fargo had indeed caught glimpses of the passengers being thrown about like rag dolls in a terrier's mouth, but short of shooting the horses—an option Fargo kept open— there would be no stopping them. Harley Doyle had been right—those wild horses were like broncos coming out of the chute, and there was apparently no end to their bottom. Their eyes showed all whites, a sure sign they were literally running in blind terror.

About halfway to Domingo Fargo saw a timbered ridge rising to the right of the trail. Instinct warned him it spelled trouble, and seconds later a round snapped only inches past his head.

Firing back was pointless and Fargo immediately employed a Cheyenne defensive tactic, letting most of his body slide down the left side of the Ovaro, holding on by the horn and one leg. Fortunately the breakneck pace quickly put the ridge behind both Fargo and the coach. But as Fargo heaved himself back into the saddle he felt a ball of ice replace his stomach.

About a quarter mile ahead, disaster loomed. The stage road made a sharp bend to the right to avoid a jagged, rocky spine.

Fargo slewed around in the saddle. "Booger! Can you turn 'em or should I shoot the leaders?"

Booger had seen how Fargo was just fired upon and realized they were still in sight of the ambushers—two dead shots. And the near-miss back at San Felipe proved that Lomax, as they neared Santa Fe, had put more killers on the job. This was no place to stop dead in their tracks, and Booger knew it.

"We all gotta die once, catfish!" he roared back. "Drop back here and haze 'em through!"

Fargo sheathed his Henry. Then he tugged left rein and hauled in a bit, positioning himself and the Ovaro close to the nearside leader as the bend loomed closer. By sheer dint of muscle and will, hauling hard on the reins and pushing forward as much as he dared on the brake, Booger managed to slow the team slightly and get them pointed into the turn. But the momentum and weight of the coach pulled against them, and despite Fargo and the Ovaro's best efforts, the terrified leaders refused to be hazed.

"Booger!" a desperate Fargo shouted as the swift wagon threatened to career out of control. "Flip me the double-ten!"

The top of the box seat lifted to provide a storage compartment. Booger somehow managed to stay on his feet as he rose up, threw the seat up and snatched out the express gun. He tossed it to Fargo, who caught it by the barrels in one hand. But just as Fargo caught it, the two offside wheels of the coach left the road as the Concord started tilting into a rollover!

The passengers screamed and shouted in terror, and Fargo felt his abject helplessness. It was too late to shoot the team. That coach had lost the desperate fight against gravity and centrifugal force, and its destruction was certain—to everyone present except Booger McTeague, master reinsman.

The foulmouthed, irreverent driver would tease and harass his passengers mercilessly, but Fargo knew he secretly harbored a sense of sacred obligation about their safety. He proved it now in a reckless and daring maneuver—as the right side of the coach started to lift, he wrapped the reins around the brake, loosed a war whoop, and leaped to the edge of the roof.

He grabbed the luggage rail and flung his prodigious bulk over, hanging down like an anchor to counterbalance the coach. It teetered on the feather edge of going over, then crashed back down onto all four wheels.

Booger had done his job and done it heroically. But now it was time for Fargo to pitch into the game or all was lost. The now driverless team had edged off the trail and were only inches away from pulling the coach onto that jagged spine of rocks. Fargo pulled both hammers of the scattergun to full cock and laid the breech against the nearside leader's head, keeping the muzzles pointed straight ahead.

He discharged both barrels. The recoil from the powerful express gun almost jerked Fargo's arm off. More importantly, the two-barreled blast terrorized the leaders back onto the trail and through the bend. With Ashton pushing up on the soles of his boots, Booger climbed aboard again and took over the reins.

He brandished a meaty fist at Fargo. "Trailsman, this is all your doing, you pearly-toothed, quiff-eating son of a motherless goat! I've lost my flask and my eating 'baccy! If I survive this day, I will unscrew your head and *shit* in it!"

Any good horse learns to feel with its rider, and over the years the Ovaro had developed the ability to sense Fargo's urgency. It was this ability that prevented the wildly plunging team from racing right past the Domingo station.

When the low adobe building came into view, Booger did his best with brake and reins, but only managed to slow the scrubs slightly. Fargo, again crowding the nearside leader, was attempting without much success to blindfold the resistant horse. It was then that the Ovaro, acting as master stallion, stretched his head across and bit down hard on the leader's neck, an act of domination that finally halted the wild ride.

The now subdued team followed the Ovaro into the wagon yard as a bloodred sun began its descent below the horizon. Fargo, fearing the worst, lit down and hurried to swing down the step, throwing the coach doors open.

"You folks all right?" he asked, his tone anxious.

"Some sore heads and minor bruises," Ashton reported. "I have a slight nosebleed. But I'll nominate you and McTeague as heroes for getting us here alive."

Fargo handed a clearly shaken Kathleen and Trixie down. Ashton and the preacher were slow to climb out, and a still petrified Malachi Feldman refused to move. Booger was forced to pluck him out and set him on his feet, supporting him as the travelers entered the station.

Fargo noticed that Booger was walking awkwardly. "You get hurt back there, old son?"

Booger, pulling off his buckskin gloves, leaned in close to Fargo and lowered his voice. "Keep this dark from the rest, catfish, but old Booger shit his pants when that rig commenced to roll over. I'll join you shortly."

Domingo station was clean but in poor repair. Here and there plaster had cracked and fallen, exposing the lathing beneath. A stove with nickel trimmings dominated the large main room. Two small Mexican boys, around eight and ten years old, watched the new arrivals with shy curiosity.

"Bienvenidos," a plump Mexican woman in a clean white apron greeted them. "Welcome. Your meal will soon be ready."

Fargo saw a big, soft-bellied Mexican man standing near the table watching him. Fargo nodded in greeting. "You must be the station master?"

"Francisco Armijo, senor. This is my *esposa*, Margarita, and *mis hijos*, Chico and Miguelito."

The two boys giggled when Fargo solemnly shook hands with each of them.

"You fellows shaving yet?" he asked, and they giggled again.

"Been any trouble around here?" Fargo asked the station master.

Armijo removed his hat and began to improve on the crease. "Trouble, senor? *De que tipo*?"

"Oh, say . . . any strangers who don't belong here been poking around?"

Armijo shook his head. "No trouble."

Margarita was serving malmsey, a sweet wine, to the still-shaken passengers. She studiously avoided Fargo's eyes.

Interesting, he thought. He cast his eye around making sure no one was lurking in the corner shadows, but the place appeared empty except for the Armijo family and the new arrivals. He kept a close watch on the front door and two doors leading off the main room.

Booger lumbered in from the yard, walking normally now. "Ha-ho, ha-ho! Margarita, where's the eats? Old Booger's backbone is scraping against his ribs. And I'll not drink that vile, womanish potation—me and Fargo will drink whiskey like men!"

"*Sí*, Senor Booger. Your usual bottle is on the table. I will bring the food now."

Fargo and Booger sat down at the table. "What do you know about Francisco?" Fargo muttered.

"Why, he's all right for a beaner, I s'pose. Good family man and a hard worker. Honest to the bone, I'd say. Spends money on masses for his soul and can name all them saints."

"Why do you figure he has trouble looking me in the eye?"

Booger narrowed his eyes. "No need to be coy, catfish. You wunner if he's been paid to fall in with killers, hey?"

Fargo glanced at the two boys, who sat on the floor playing with a spinning top.

"For a man who loves his family," he replied, "money wouldn't be the main motivation."

Booger put his bottle back down, letting this point sink in. Now he watched Armijo, who had crossed to the bar in the corner. "Well, I'll be dawg."

"What?"

"Watch him."

Fargo saw the station master take down a drink fast, then pour himself another.

"I ain't never seen him touch liquor," Booger said. "Now he's a damn bucket belly like me. It don't cipher."

Senora Armijo came out from the kitchen carrying a huge serving tray. She began to set out steaming bowls of tamales and *menudo*.

"Francisco!" Booger called out. "C'mere a minute."

The station master crossed reluctantly to the table. He started a smile and then abandoned the effort, trapped by Fargo's and Booger's stares. "Yes?"

"Is there something you need to tell us?" Fargo said mildly.

Clearly Armijo was gnawing himself inside over something. "*Nada*, senor," he replied, his face sweating profusely.

Booger ripped the corn husk off a tamale. He was about to pop the entire thing into his mouth when Fargo suddenly slapped it out of his hand.

"H'ar now, you little runt! How'd you like to wear your ass for a hat?"

Fargo stared at Margarita, who was on the verge of tears. "The food is poisoned, isn't it?"

She nodded, and now the tears did come like a dam bursting. At this intelligence, every face at the table went a few shades paler.

"Only your food and Booger's has been poisoned, Senor Fargo," Armijo confessed, his face crumpling into a mask of abject misery. "With hemlock. God forgive me!"

"Settle down and have a seat," Fargo said. "Some gringo came here with the poison, right? Told you he'd kill your family if you didn't cooperate?"

"*Preciso*. This is the truth, *lo juro*—I swear it! He said *mis hijos* would be killed if I did not do this thing. We are *Mexicanos*, Senor Fargo—the gringo law does not protect us. And out here, *pues*, there *is* no law."

Fargo nodded. "You did it out of fear for your family. I'd likely do the same thing in your place. You have my word, Francisco—no one is going to hurt your boys. Now tell me—did you know the man?"

Armijo shook his head. "Never did I see him before. He was a man perhaps your age wearing fine clothing. His head was—*como se dice?*—with little hair."

"Bald?"

"Yes, this. A face a man quickly forgets."

"It doesn't matter—they're all one. Margarita, I'm famished—are you *sure* only these two plates are poisoned?"

"*Claro.* Pick any plate and I will eat from it."

"I believe you. Toss this stuff and knock us up some safe grub, wouldja? The rest of you go ahead and eat."

"Senor Fargo," Armijo said, producing a yellow telegram flimsy from his pocket. "This *telegrapho* was brought today by a messenger from the new *estacion de telegrafiar* at Cerrillos."

"It's from Addison Steele in El Paso," Fargo said, unfolding it and reading it aloud. " 'Have identified possible Lomax informer at this end. Judd Moates, Assistant Division Manager, was reported by Commerce Bank after depositing one thousand dollars. Moates has not confessed but cannot explain such a large sum of money. Other Overland employees may be compromised.' "

Fargo loosed a fluming sigh. "This might have been useful ten days ago when we were wondering if Lomax knew what stage Kathleen was taking. Talk about closing the barn door after the horse escapes."

"Aye," Booger said, staring toward Ashton. "And seeing's how Lomax knew which run she was on, nothing stopped him from placing a man on it."

"Nothing at all," Ashton agreed. "And it's clear both of you suspect me."

"Let's just say we have an eye on you," Fargo said. "And on everyone else."

"Even me?" Trixie said.

Fargo grinned. "Even you, dear heart."

Domingo was not a layover station. With a fresh relay they would travel on that night to Cochiti Lake, the last full station before Santa Fe, where they would spend the last night of this treacherous journey. All that remained, after Cochiti Lake, was a swing station at Burro Bluff.

But Fargo knew damn well—with tomorrow being the fateful deadline of June nineteenth—that the worst trouble in the world awaited them, and the longest miles still lay ahead.

16

Blood Mesa, a red rock table pockmarked with tiny caves, was located ten miles west of Santa Fe, its southern face only about two hundred yards from the Overland stage road. Eons of exposure to the harsh elements had darkened the rock to the exact shade of dried blood and earned it its name. Shortly after dark on the night of June eighteenth, Zack Lomax and his lackey Olney Lucas pitched a cold camp in the lee of the mesa's northern face.

"The horses are hid real good in a barranca close by," Olney reported, returning to the fire. "You can't see them from the road."

"Good," Lomax said. "Build me a smoke."

Lomax had not relaxed since their arrival. He rocked from his heels to his toes, too wrought up to remain still.

"We won't know until tomorrow what happened at Domingo," he repeated yet again. "Did you have the impression this Armijo would do as ordered?"

"He seemed scared, all right, when I brought his kids into it. It bothers me, though, that he wouldn't accept any money."

"Yes, damn it! You can't trust a man like that. But you know how these Mexicans are about their families."

The wind had howled and roared since their arrival, buffeting them even in the lee of the mesa, and Lomax finally gave up trying to light his cigarette.

"At any rate," he added, "Ridley is far more predictable. He'd gut his own grandmother for a plugged peso, and I'm certain he'll pass the word along at Cochiti Lake station."

"Speaking of that, boss," Olney put in, "it's too late for me to spill the beans to anybody. Can't you tell me who you hired to ride the coach?"

"Yes, I suppose there's no risk now. Have you ever heard of a man named Clement Majors?"

Olney loosed a sharp whistle. "You don't mean the assassin they call 'the Undertaker'?"

"Oh, don't I? Have you ever known me to do things on the cheap?"

"I'm impressed, boss. They say he's killed more than forty men and eluded lawmen from the Rio to the Tetons. The newspapers claim he's as savage as a meat axe."

"A meat axe? That's drawing it mild. Later tonight he should know the final plan."

"He better be as good as he's painted because Fargo definitely is. I never thought he'd make it so far."

"I'm not at all surprised at Fargo's success," Lomax said. "He's obviously one of those men who can concentrate the purpose of a group."

Lomax began pacing around the fire. "Actually, that's one trait Fargo and I share in common. There's at least one more: We've both spent so much time alone that we don't think like the majority. That makes the bastard totally unpredictable."

Lomax was silent for a full minute, anger roiling his guts as memory flexed a muscle and again put him back in San Francisco, one year ago, when all his ambitions for controlling California had suffered a miscarriage—all because of a haughty, stuck-up bitch who acted like her shit didn't stink.

"I'm going to balance the ledger, Olney, do you see that?" he demanded, his voice tightening an octave in his resentment. "One year tomorrow, and in all this time since that day I've had nothing else on my mind. She thought she was turning a bull into a steer, but she thought wrong. Tomorrow I'm going to gut that bitch—I'll carve her goddamn stone heart out of her chest and preserve it in brine!"

It irritated Olney when a man poured out his guts like this without shame. It was a sign of Lomax's obsession and insanity, this need to plough old ground over and over like the mindless repetition of a parrot. He considered Lomax a crazy, pigheaded son of a bitch and didn't care a rat's ass about his vendetta against some high-toned actress.

However, two hundred dollars a month, when most men were lucky to earn thirty, kept him loyal. But good salary or no, if the Undertaker didn't take control from Fargo by the time that Concord reached Blood Mesa late tomorrow, Olney was lighting a shuck out of the territory.

Lomax finally settled down on a rock in front of the fire. "It's like this Olney—a man with a mortal grudge has only two choices: either end it or mend it. And as of tonight, it's past mending."

Fargo knew the fat was in the fire now, and he was taking no chances.

Although bone weary, he and Booger sacrificed any sleep that night. Both remained on sentry duty, one walking the grounds of Cochiti station while the other sat outside of the room where Kathleen and Trixie slept. Several times Fargo engaged the station master, Ridley Spencer, in conversation, trying to get a read on him. But the man had a face like a wooden Indian and was too taciturn—or wary—to draw out.

Fargo had ordered all the passengers to take no food or drink except from the pump outside. Ashton, Malachi and the preacher, beat out from their wild ride, had all curled up in blankets on pallets in the center of the main room. It troubled him that he couldn't keep a constant eye on them, but each time he checked, all three appeared to be enjoying the sleep of the just.

"Well, catfish," Booger said when he joined Fargo just after sunrise, "quiet all damn night. That's bad medicine. 'Pears to me Lomax and his shit-jobbers plan to brace us on the last stage. And it's perfect country for killers."

Fargo nodded, rising from his chair to stretch the kinks from his back. "The way you say. Lomax ain't about to show the white feather now—not after all he's put into this deal."

"We ain't the only ones didn't sleep last night," Booger said, nodding toward the door behind Fargo. "I heard sheets rustling in there, and don't seem likely it was Trixie. Her Nibs is scairt."

"She's scared in her flesh but stout in her spirit. But it's not just her that needs to fret. Won't any of us be able to rest easy until Lomax is planted in the bone orchard."

Booger scowled. "I'd lay odds there's at least one that ain't scairt. And damn your eyes, Fargo, you lanky yack!

You know I am fond to foolishness of my eating 'baccy, and none to be had. Now you starve me of victuals. I say let's eat Feldman—the little piss squirt is useless and he'd make a crackerjack pot roast."

Fargo grinned. "Take too long to cook him. Roust everybody out and let's raise dust. There's trouble ahead and I'm keen for sport."

"Aye, today you'll get my life over, eh? It's been your wish all along, you treacherous, evil son of a bitch. Well, at least old Booger got to see Her Nibs naked."

The swift wagon, running behind a fresh team of Cleveland bays, pulled out a half hour later. Fargo again rode roving point on the Ovaro, roaming out ahead to scout for trouble but staying within sight of the coach. The terrain now was rugged and dangerous, the Overland route winding into the foothills of the Sangre de Cristo mountains to the east, a major southern range of the Rockies. Pine trees grew in thick clusters, excellent nests for snipers.

Toward midmorning he looped back to ride alongside the Concord. "How long before we hit the swing station at Burro Bluff?" he asked Booger.

"Two hours." Booger tried to spit on him, but without the weight of tobacco juice the wind blew it back onto his shirt. Booger cursed. "Damn you to hell, Fargo! No whiskey, no 'baccy, no eats—I oughter pound you to paste!"

"Old son, you hold a grudge until it hollers 'mama.'"

Every time Fargo returned to the coach, he could feel the weight of Lansford Ashton's stare like a hand on his neck. The rest of the passengers seemed to be dazed, the cumulative result of a long, grueling stagecoach trip, gnawing hunger, and their near-death experience yesterday.

Again Fargo spurted ahead, tempting any shooters and fully aware that Russ Alcott and his partner were both expert marksmen. As the hours passed, however, without any eruption of violence, his apprehension increased. They could easily have opened up by now, and the fact that they hadn't hinted ominously of some major change in tactics. Fargo preferred the devil he knew over the one he didn't.

They reached Burro Bluff without incident. There had been no attacks on the horses here, further convincing Fargo that some new travail awaited them. Booger had hitched his thoughts to the same post.

"Christ on a crutch!" he groused as the swingman harnessed the new relay. "How's come they're waiting so damn long?"

Fargo shrugged one shoulder, eyes scanning the timbered slopes above the station. "It's always possible we wore 'em down. Maybe Lomax figured that poison would do for us back at Domingo."

"You're talkin' out the back of your neck," Booger scoffed. "We got hard ground ahead."

"I expect so," Fargo agreed. "As I recall, the stretch known as the Narrows is about an hour ahead of us."

Booger nodded, his face grim. That five-mile stretch of trail, called *Los Estrechos* by the Mexican locals, was a favorite lure to road agents of every stripe. It was a series of long, serpentine cut banks through solid granite bluffs—cut banks formed by eons of drainage from the cordillera of nearby mountains.

"Aye, the Narrows. A God-forgotten stretch where hell has been turned inside out. Once into it, catfish, there's no escape routes in any direction, not even on foot. And the mouse that has but one hole is quickly taken. With killers laying for us, I'd as lief smell a sheepherder's socks as ride the Narrows."

"All right, folks!" Fargo called to the passengers. "Pile in. We got to git."

"We're close now, right, Skye?" Trixie asked in a plaintive voice.

"Mighty close. The next stop is Santa Fe right around sunset."

"Thank the Lord!" she said, her tone buoyant now. "There's been no trouble so far today."

When Fargo met Kathleen's eyes, however, he saw that her thoughts matched his: it was too damn soon to tack up bunting. As Booger started to heave his bulk onto the box, Fargo stepped in close and put a hand on his shoulder. He lowered his voice.

"If anybody inside that coach is going to make some kind of a play," he told his friend, "he has to do it quick now. I'm

148

staying beside the coach until we hit the Narrows. Booger, it's up and on the line now for both of us. We couldn't see what those passengers were doing every minute back at Cochiti. I don't trust that station master, either. There's a damn good chance he relayed some kind of plan to one of them. We have to be ready for any damn thing."

Booger nodded solemnly. "We have to watch for a pincers, that's the gait. A move from within the coach just as a shitstorm starts from outside. Catfish, if we are on the cusp of death, won't you at least ask Trixie if I might see her naked? *Our* asses are hanging in the wind, why shouldn't hers?"

Fargo burst out laughing. "You do measure corn by your own bushel, don't you? Never mind the foofaraw. We make it to Santa Fe, I promise you can screw yourself into a slight limp and I'll post the pony for it."

"So? If I sacrifice the meat you'll buy me the mustard, hey? It's the bastards with pretty teeth I must watch for—they piss down my back and swear it's only raining."

Still complaining bitterly, Booger climbed onto the box and cracked his whip, setting the team in motion. Fargo forked leather and rode alongside the coach.

Again Ashton met his eyes. "Getting a bit nervous, Fargo?"

Fargo's hard blue stare finally made Ashton avert his gaze.

"Nothing a quick, clean kill won't take care of, Mr. Ashton," he finally replied.

17

"Fargo," Booger called down to him, "you best hark to our front trail now. There's the Narrows dead ahead."

"I'll ride ahead and take a squint around," Fargo said. "Why don't you stay put until I give the hail?"

Booger knew exactly what he meant. He reined in the team, set the brake, and pulled the express gun out from the box seat compartment. He climbed down and took up a stance beside the coach, first loosening his dragoon pistol in its holster. If he fired into that stagecoach, it wouldn't be with a scattergun.

Fargo knew this stretch was too long to scout completely in one fell swoop. He figured to take it a mile at a time, stopping the coach each time. It would throw them off schedule, but there was no help for it. He couldn't leave those passengers unguarded in this ambushers' paradise.

Fargo hadn't ridden more than fifteen minutes before he fully realized the daunting odds he was up against if jumped here. The road, hemmed in tight by rock faces, random basalt turrets, and innumerable rock tumbles, defied even careful scouting. Soon it turned into a tortuous crinkum-crankum with blind spots at many of the turns. Every spot that presented itself was potential death. He resorted to his only hope: careful attention to warnings from the Ovaro.

The stallion didn't like this deathtrap any better than Fargo did. Several times he stutter-stepped sideways when wind gusts shrieked through the rock formations, and he fought the bit when Fargo kneed him forward again. Slowly and steadily, however, they wended their way through the Narrows, and the ever-expected gunshots never rang out.

Sweat beaded on Fargo's forehead but dried instantly in the hot, arid wind. He finished the first mile and fired a shot into the air, calling the rig forward.

"That first part is the most dangersome," Booger said when the coach rolled up. "Happens them curly wolves wanted to cut us down here, they'd likely a done it by now. Why'n't we just roll behind you for the rest? We'll be here until nightfall if we keep going piecemeal."

Fargo checked the slant of the shadows to gauge the time. Then he nodded. "It's a mite risky, maybe, but seeing's how scouting is limited here anyhow, let's keep our firepower concentrated."

Booger hooked a thumb down toward the coach. "Uh-hunh. Concentrated, catfish." So Fargo altered his tactics and stayed close as the swift wagon rolled on, close enough to keep a vigilant eye on the interior of the coach. Kathleen sat demurely by herself in her reserved rear seat, her face pale and drawn. Ashton and Pastor Brandenburg occupied the middle seat, Trixie and Malachi the seat behind the driver.

Fargo also continued to carefully study the terrain on both sides of the stage road. Booger was right: as they progressed farther into the Narrows the wild landscape tamed somewhat, and the Ovaro had settled down considerably. In less than an hour they debouched into more open territory.

"Well, I'm a Dutchman!" Booger exclaimed. "Old Booger was certain-sure they'd pour it to us back there. Long-shanks, mayhap you was right. Could be that Lomax had big plans for that poison back at Domingo. If the sick son of a bitch means to make his play, he'd best do it quick. Hell, it's a straight shot now to Santa Fe."

"Sure, but maybe he's counting on us thinking just like you are right now. Like I said, Booger, it's best all the way around if they *do* make their big play on the trail. Today's June nineteenth, Lomax's big day, and if he decides he still means to kill Kathleen, it's best we *know* the day he means to try it. Once this day passes, he's still going to kill her, but we won't know where or when. Santa Fe is a big town, hoss."

"That shines," Booger agreed. "Damn, I hope Her Nibs

will at least give old Booger a pair of frilly step-ins if we put the kibosh on Lomax. I seen a real purty pair when that trunk o' hers fell off in the road."

"I heard that, Mr. McTeague," she called out the window. "You can have them as a peace offering."

Booger's jaw slacked open in shock, and Fargo laughed. "Just push the dainties from your thoughts and keep a weather eye out. I still say we got a nasty frolic coming up soon."

But still the afternoon wore on, uneventful, the rig making good time.

"Blood Mesa ahead," Booger announced. "Only ten miles to Santa Fe now."

Fargo had known of Blood Mesa for years, considering it little more than a distinctive landmark when he approached Santa Fe from the west. Now, however, he paid it more attention as it loomed just ahead of them on the left.

"Stop the rig, Booger," he called out. "I want to look at that mesa before we roll past it."

Fargo was about to gig the Ovaro forward when a sharp, feminine gasp from inside the coach arrested him. Fargo glanced inside and realized the fandango had arrived at last.

The "preacher's" big clasp Bible now lay open on the seat beside him, showing how the pages had been hollowed out inside it. And the gun that had been secreted there, a Colt Pocket Model, was now pressed firmly to Kathleen's left temple.

"End of the trail, Fargo," Clement Majors announced calmly. "Now *all* of you do exactly what I tell you, or America's Sweetheart gets an airshaft through her pretty little head."

Fargo sat still as stone in the saddle. Booger, unaware of what was happening inside the coach, cursed impatiently.

"The hell you waiting on, Fargo, a Chinook?" he demanded.

"We got us a little problem, Booger," Fargo replied, nodding toward the passengers. "Just sit still and don't make a play."

"A wise course of action," the man known as the Undertaker approved. "I'm not alone, Fargo. This coach is under the guns right now, and the men drawing their beads shoot straight as plumb lines. That fat ape on the box makes for an easy target."

"So *here's* the cock o' the dung heap!" Booger exclaimed, recognizing the voice. "Skye, I hated that son of a bitch preacher from the get-go. But them perfumed side whiskers throwed me off the scent."

"Fargo," Majors instructed, "light down slowly. Use your left hand to unbuckle that shell belt and drop it in the trail. Then raise your hands high and take five steps back from your horse. *That's* the ticket, slow and steady. Ashton, toss that valise out the window and then step outside the coach. Then Trixie, then Malachi."

When everyone was assembled, Majors pushed Kathleen out of the coach in front of him. "McTeague," he called out. "You stay right where you are. But toss down your rifle, six-gun, and the express gun. I also want those two firearms Fargo liberated from the man back at San Felipe."

"They want ice water in hell, too," Booger growled. In his anger his neck swelled and his face turned red.

"Do what the man told you," Fargo ordered. "This is his show now."

Majors grinned. "Finally the great Trailsman shows a spark of intelligence. All these past ten days you've strained at gnats while swallowing camels."

"That's too rich for my belly—spell it out."

"It's just a biblical way we *preachers* have of telling you you're a fool. All along you suspected Ashton and dismissed me as a Bible-thumping irritant."

"That was pretty stupid of me," Fargo agreed amiably.

"Indeed. But most men *are* stupid compared to me."

Fargo noticed Ashton inching toward his valise.

"Never mind, Ashton," Fargo said. "That gun ain't worth a kiss my ass. I pulled the firing pin while you were sleeping."

Majors laughed, enjoying himself immensely. "Lomax!" he suddenly roared out at the top of his lungs. "All secure! You and the others can come down now!"

Now, the Colt's muzzle pressed tight against Kathleen's temple, he looked at each passenger in turn as if inspecting them. "You, Ashton," he said, "are all right in my books. You, too, Trixie. As for you, Malachi . . ."

The astrological doctor's face drained white at mention of his name.

"There's nothing a *real* man out west fears more than being thought a coward. Look how calmly Fargo is facing his inevitable demise. You, however, wear your white liver on your sleeve. Killing you will embarrass me—you aren't worth the bullet."

Kathleen finally spoke up, her voice reedy with fright. "You can't mean you're going to kill *all* of us?"

"I'm afraid Zack Lomax has insisted on it, and wisely so. You can't leave witnesses in an affair of this kind. Your mistake, Miss Barton, was in trusting Skye Fargo to save you. Neither his fighting skills nor his courage are in question—but as he proved by pulling Ashton's firing pin, he's not of the requisite mental caliber."

By now Fargo could see two men—Alcott and the man who had sided him in the ambush from the ridge—slowly picking their way down the face of Blood Mesa. Two more men had just rounded the east side of the mesa, bearing toward the stagecoach. Fargo estimated he had about four minutes now.

"I won't play the Janus face and say I won't enjoy killing all of you," Majors added. "Enjoyment is why I went into this line, you see. There is an almost transcendent thrill in watching the vital light in my victim's eyes turn to a glassy stare as they give up the ghost—as the vital élan dissipates like smoke in a breeze and a 'human being' turns into a puppet made of meat."

"You're mighty fond of stumping," Fargo remarked. "Maybe you *shoulda* been a preacher. Or is this just your usual line of blather before you murder?"

"I forgive your sarcasm, Trailsman. You must be embarrassed, for it would appear your highly vaunted powers of observation and deduction have failed you miserably. Why else would you focus on Ashton, an innocent man, and fail to realize I was your arch nemesis?"

Again Fargo checked the progress of the men approaching the stage.

"Actually," he replied, "I suspected you, too. My problem was trying to decide if the two of you were a team."

"Do tell? Then you should have acted on that suspicion."

"Oh, I did. See, I began to ask myself why a preacher would haul around a big, five-pound Bible and never once open it and read from it. So one night when you were asleep, I took a little peek inside and found the gun."

Majors chuckled. "I see now why you're reputed to be such a fine poker player. But the bluff won't work—I can see that my firing pin is still intact, and there's a bullet in each chamber."

"Oh, I didn't touch the firing pin. That trick with the Bible made it clear you ain't no green-antler. But you see, 'Preacher,' I always carry crimping pliers in my gear. It was only a few minutes work to pry off the bullets, dump the powder loads, and crimp the shells again. Because, you see, I realized I just might be up against the master assassin known as the Undertaker."

For the first time Majors' sneer of cold command seemed to waver. "Nice try, Fargo, quite commendable. But I'll give the lie to it right now."

He quickly pointed the gun at Malachi and squeezed the trigger. There was only a muted pop as the primer load detonated.

The realization that Fargo had foxed him struck Majors like a home punch. But Fargo didn't wait to see if the killer would resort to a second hideout gun. In one smooth, fluid movement, he raised his right leg, plucked the Arkansas toothpick from its boot sheath, and threw it hard into Majors' vitals. A rope of blood spurted over his lip as he collapsed in a lifeless heap.

"Quick now!" Fargo ordered. "All of you do exactly what I tell you. We have to play this deal just right—it *has* to end right here and right now!"

18

Fargo began pulling off his boots. "Booger," he called out. "Stay right where you are. Make sure the brake is set good. In a minute I'm going to fire five shots. The first one is going to kill me. The second one kills you. When you hear that second shot, roll *to the right* off the box, so you land back here on the blind side of the rig—and *don't* break your damn neck. Then get your rifle, cover down, and snap in."

Fargo pulled off his shirt and looked at the rest. "Then I'm going to fire three more shots to make it sound like Majors killed Trixie, Ashton and Malachi. Kathleen, nerve up because after that last shot, you and me are going to step into view. When you hear me shout to Booger, dive behind that coach and hunker down."

Fargo looked at Ashton. "Grab my Henry. When you hear me shout, open up with me and Booger. All of us have to take out Alcott and his pard first—Lomax and the jasper with him got no rifles and prob'ly can't shoot worth a damn anyhow. As soon as the two riflemen are down, shoot those other two to doll stuffings."

By now Fargo was pulling off his buckskin trousers, and he grinned when neither woman bothered to avert their eyes—and, in fact, stared at his sex as if mesmerized.

Ashton had already twigged the game and started pulling the dead assassin's black clergy garb off him. Fargo hurriedly put on the suit and donned the battered homburg.

"Get set, Booger," Fargo said, firing his first shot into the ground. At the second shot, the coach rocked hard as Booger rolled off as if shot, cursing in a low voice when he hit the ground hard.

"God rot your soul, Fargo, I've broken my ass bone!"

Fargo fired three more shots. "All right, you two," he said to Booger and Ashton, "get set. Malachi and Trixie, get flat and don't move."

He stuffed his Colt into the waistband of the trousers, hidden behind the coat. Then he turned to Kathleen. "Ready?"

She swallowed a lump of fear and nodded. "Ready. This is worse than stage fright."

Fargo, keeping his head turned to the side to hide his beard, led her out in front of the team. By now the four advancing men were within easy range. Fargo knew he had to time this perfectly—let them get as close as possible before one of them got suspicious, then open fire before they could fully react.

"Yes, the one wearing the fancy embroidered vest is Lomax," Kathleen confirmed in a voice just above a whisper.

Fargo chanced a quick glance. Lomax, demented triumph clear in his face, wore a six-gun in a flap holster, but it was the dagger he carried that arrested Fargo's attention. Even in the day's fading sunlight the jewel-encrusted silver hilt gave off sparkles of light.

"That dagger is for me," Kathleen said grimly.

"I got something for him, too," Fargo vowed.

"Congratulations, Clement!" Lomax shouted. "I see it pays to hire the best! Are they all dead?"

Fargo nodded. But his failure to turn and face the other men squarely finally alerted Alcott. "It's a trap!" he shouted. "That's Fargo!"

"Now!" Fargo shouted, giving Kathleen a hard push to safety when she failed to move fast enough.

It was over quicker than Booger could swallow a biscuit. Two rifles and a handgun opened up with sustained ferocity, and Alcott and the man siding him went down without firing a shot. Lomax dropped the dagger and was clawing his sidearm out when one of Fargo's bullets punched into his forehead, knocking him out from under his hat. The man beside him broke into a panicked run, but Booger's big-bore North & Savage cut him down.

Fargo never took chances with possum players. He took the Henry from Ashton and pumped a finishing shot into each man's head—even a second bullet for Lomax.

"Catfish, I oughter baste your bacon!" Booger growled when Fargo walked back to join the others. "How's come you didn't say word one about the gun in that Bible?"

"Because I was deliberately making the Undertaker think I only suspected Ashton. You can't give a killer like that the slightest clue. And if you woulda known, the way you hated him already, you would likely have killed him before we learned where the trap was set. And I wasn't about to let Lomax get away."

Kathleen looked like a woman who had just harrowed hell. "Is it over, Skye?" she said in a wondering tone. "Is it really over?"

"It's over, lady. The sick bastard is dead as a Paiute grave—Christ!"

Luckily Fargo was just in time to catch her when America's Sweetheart fainted dead away.

The Bella Union was packed beyond capacity for the opening of *To Love No Other* starring America's Sweetheart, Kathleen Barton. "Her finest performance to date!" a noted critic would rave the next day in the *Santa Fe New Mexican*. "Her impassioned soliloquy, in the final act, on the fragility of life did not seem like 'acting' at all—rather, it seemed to emanate from the heart of one who had crossed to 'Death's other kingdom' and somehow managed to return against all odds."

But the famous actress, claiming a headache, had foregone the usual gathering of actors and theater luminaries that usually followed a premier. Earlier that day she had sent personal invitations to the five individuals who had recently accompanied her on a ten-day ascent into hell; she requested their presence in her lavish suite of rooms at the famous Dorsey House in the heart of Santa Fe.

The finest liquors and food delicacies had been laid out on long tables in her drawing room. The attending porter gawked in sheer amazement when a buckskin-clad frontiersman, accompanied by a man the size of the Comstock Lode, entered the suite.

"Ha-ho, ha-ho!" Booger bellowed out, seizing a Cornish hen and devouring half of it in one bite. He glowered at

Malachi Feldman. "A good thing there's plenty of victuals, you little pop-eyed freak, for I'm still sorely tempted to eat you."

Ashton met Fargo's eyes and both men grinned. Shortly after their safe arrival in Santa Fe, Fargo had apologized to Ashton for his suspicion of him during the journey from El Paso. Fargo's contrition, however, hadn't prevented him from cleaning out Ashton at poker earlier that day.

Kathleen, demure and lovely in a pinch-waisted gown that left her slim shoulders bare and lifted her breasts provocatively, turned to Trixie. "Miss Belle, have you taken your position at the, ah, thirst parlor?"

"Yes, I start singing tomorrow at La Paloma on Palace Avenue."

"Fine, but if I have my way, that truly fine voice of yours won't be wasted in some smelly saloon. I've arranged for you to audition for Mr. John Lofton, director of the Bella Union. With just a bit of study I'm convinced you can become a fine operatic singer. And then you can indeed 'paddle your own canoe.'"

Booger, who was searching in vain for a bottle of whiskey fit for a man, looked almost as surprised and grateful as Trixie. "Why, Your Haughtiness, what a fine—"

"And *you*, Mr. McTeague," Kathleen cut him off in a scolding tone. "You are undoubtedly the most disgusting pig I have ever met. The stench blowing off you could stop the Armada. You are a stain upon the code of chivalry and an affront to decent women everywhere."

Booger's eyes suddenly misted. "Aww, muffin, I ain't got the words to answer that fine praise."

"You are also," she added, "strong, fearless and indomitable. I shall never—God help me—forget you. As promised, these 'frillies' are for you."

She plucked a small carton off the table and handed it to him. Then she stretched up—*way* up—on tiptoes and kissed the man-mountain on his wind-cracked lips. Fargo and Ashton goggled as if a dog had just recited Shakespeare.

"As for *you*, Trailsman," she said, turning that achingly beautiful face toward Fargo, "I'll be staying right here for the next six weeks. I shall be absolutely heartbroken if you don't stop by to . . . visit before you ride off on your next, no-doubt reckless escapade."

"That goes double for me, Skye," Trixie put in, fluttering her lashes. "I'm staying at the Alameda."

Fargo touched the brim of his hat to both women. He opened his mouth to reply to this embarrassment of riches, but Booger beat him to it.

"Yes, we know, catfish: 'With me it's always the lady's choice.'"

"Pah!" Fargo shot back, and the room erupted in laughter.

LOOKING FORWARD!
The following is the opening section of the next novel in the exciting Trailsman series from Signet:

TRAILSMAN #377
BOUNTY HUNT

A town deep in the Rockies, 1861—where outlaws ruled the roost, and life came cheap.

Skye Fargo wasn't expecting trouble. He'd been riding for days to reach the town of Meridian, and once he was over a high pass he'd have only six or seven miles to go.

It was midmorning when he reached the top of Bald Peak and the cleft that would take him from one side of the range to the other.

That high up, the air was cool, even in the summer. A hawk circled over the timber and a raven eyed him from a roost in a tree.

The pass was a cleft with high walls, wide enough for a wagon. It was like riding through a tunnel without a roof.

Out of habit, Fargo rode with his hand on his Colt.

This was wild country. The Shadow Mountains, as they were called, were the haunt of hostiles and outlaws. The unwary paid for being careless with their lives.

Fargo had lived too long on the raw edge to let his guard

down. So it was that as he came to the end of the pass, he drew rein to scan the slopes below.

A big man, wide at the shoulders and narrow at the hips, Fargo wore buckskins and a white hat nearly brown from the dust of many miles. His eyes were as blue as a high-country lake. His face was flint-hard, and uncommonly pleasing to the female eye. One look at him and most folks realized he wasn't the sort of hombre you tangled with if you were in your right mind.

But someone decided to.

Fargo glimpsed a flash of light near a cluster of giant rock slabs. He'd seen similar flashes before—the gleam of sunlight off metal. Hunching forward, Fargo used his spurs. The Ovaro exploded into motion just as a shot cracked and a leaden bee buzzed his ear. Drawing the Colt, Fargo fired at the slabs even as he reined sharply to the right.

He needed to hunt cover. Except for scattered boulders, the ground was open to the tree line, making it easy to pick a rider off. Or so the bushwhacker no doubt hoped.

Bent low over his saddle horn, Fargo galloped hard.

He worried the shooter would try to bring down the Ovaro. To prevent that he fired twice more to make the man hunt cover.

A large boulder loomed. It wasn't big enough to shield the Ovaro but Fargo put it between him and the rifleman to make it harder for the man to hit them.

His best hope was to reach a line of pines that came within a few hundred feet of the crest. He nearly got a cramp in his neck from looking over his shoulder for another flash of sunlight. Strangely, there wasn't any. There had just been that one shot.

Then Fargo saw why.

A man on a sorrel had broken from the cluster of slabs and was making for the forest.

Maybe his own shots had come too close for comfort, Fargo realized. Or it could be the killer figured to reach the woods first and cut him off.

Like hell, Fargo vowed. The Ovaro was second to no

other horse when it came to speed and stamina. He'd pitted the stallion against the fine mounts of the Comanche and the Sioux and in races with whites, and the Ovaro nearly always proved their better.

Pebbles clattering from under the stallion's flying hooves, Fargo made it to the pines without being shot. Once in among them, he raced down the slope, flying for more than fifty yards before common sense warned him to haul on the reins and give a listen.

The mountain had gone quiet. The bushwhacker could be anywhere.

Quietly, quickly, Fargo replaced the spent cartridges in the Colt. He added a sixth although he normally left the chamber under the hammer empty.

Shadow dappled the woodland. For that matter, much of the range was darker than usual. It was why people called them the Shadow Mountains.

Fargo gigged the stallion. He was alert for movement of any kind. Once, a hint of motion made him raise the Colt but it was only a jay taking wing.

What spooked it? Fargo wondered. Reining behind a spruce, he climbed down. He twirled the Colt into his holster, shucked his Henry rifle from the saddle scabbard and worked the lever to feed a round into the chamber.

Tucked at the knees, Fargo worked around the spruce and over to a fir. He hunkered and studied the shadows near where the jay had been. Just when he was about convinced he must be mistaken, a head and a hat poked from behind a trunk and scoured the woods in his direction.

Fargo froze. The man had a fair idea where he was but didn't know for sure. He watched as the head swung from side to side and then disappeared. At that distance he couldn't tell much other than the man had a beard a lot bushier than his own.

Fargo waited. With any luck the killer would come to him. It depended on how much the man wanted him dead.

Apparently a lot, because it wasn't a minute later that Fargo spied a figure flitting from tree to tree.

Inwardly, Fargo smiled. Slowly raising the Henry, he pressed the stock to his shoulder, his cheek to the brass, and sighted down the barrel. All he needed was a clear shot.

The man didn't give it to him. Whoever he was, the killer was always on the move and never showed more than a small part of himself.

Fargo decided to go for the chest. He saw the man dart behind an evergreen. Shifting slightly, he fixed his sights on the other side. Sure enough, the man reappeared. Fargo held his breath, and fired.

The Henry boomed and bucked and the figure plunged to the ground.

Fargo didn't go rushing down. He stalked through the vegetation until he spied a pair of legs jutting from behind a log. They were toes-up and weren't moving.

Suspicious of a trick, Fargo eased onto his belly and snaked to the log. Taking off his hat, he slowly raised his head high enough to see over.

The bushwhacker was flat on his back. Tall and lean, he had dark eyes wide in shock. His clothes were store bought and not in good condition, and his hat was pinned under his head and partially flattened. In the middle of his shirt was a spreading scarlet stain. His chest rose and fell in labored breaths, and each time he breathed out, scarlet bubbled. Pink froth rimmed his thin lips.

Jamming his own hat back on, Fargo stood and trained the Henry on his would-be killer. He stepped over the log, kicked the man's Spencer well out of reach, and snatched a Remington from a holster and tossed it after the rifle.

The man glared the whole while.

Stepping back, Fargo cradled the Henry. "What were you after? Money?"

The bushwhacker went on glaring.

"Stupid son of a bitch," Fargo said. "I've got barely ten dollars in my poke."

The man tried to speak but all that came out were puffs of breath. Gritting his blood-flecked teeth, he tried again, gasping, "Not . . . money."

"What then? My horse?" Fargo looked around. The killer's sorrel was down the slope a ways, tied to a tree.

"You've already got one."

"Not . . . horse," the man gasped.

"You tried to blow out my wick for the hell of it?" Fargo had met some who would. Human wolves with no more conscience than a rock.

"You," the bearded man said. "Kill . . . you."

Fargo's brow puckered in puzzlement. "You were waiting for *me*?"

A crafty gleam came into those beady eyes.

"Hold on," Fargo said, looking the man up and down. "I've never seen you before. Why in hell would you want to kill me?"

The man didn't answer.

Fargo was at a loss. No one knew he was coming to Meridian. Not even the person who sent for him, since he'd never answered her letter. "Who are you?"

The man glared.

"I'll make a deal," Fargo said. "Tell me what I want to know and I'll bury you. Don't, and I'll leave you for the coyotes and the buzzards." Some men wouldn't care one way or the other but he had nothing else to bargain with.

"Clemens," the man got out. "Handle . . . is Clemens."

"I'll ask you again. Why ambush me?"

"Stop . . . you," Clemens said.

"Stop me from what?" Fargo asked, and even as he did, it hit him. "To stop me from reaching town? From talking to her?"

"You do," Clemens gasped, "you die."

"Are you the reason she sent for me?"

Clemens snorted, or tried to. Crimson drops dribbled from his nose and more blood frothed his mouth. "Others will get you. *He'll* get you."

"Who?"

Closing his eyes, Clemens shuddered. His breathing became shallow and his face paled before Fargo's eyes. The man wasn't long for this world.

Fargo went through his pockets. He found twenty-two dollars in coins and a few bills, a folding knife, and a pocket watch that didn't work. It told him nothing.

Fargo retrieved the sorrel. He untied it and brought it over and looped the reins around a broken branch on the log. Then he rummaged through the saddlebags. There were spare clothes, as worn as those Clemens had on, spare socks with holes in them, cartridges, some coffee and a coffeepot, a tin cup and a fork and a fire steel and flint for starting a fire.

Turning to his would-be assassin, Fargo squatted and poked him.

Clemens opened his eyes.

"Last chance to tell me who is behind this."

"Go . . . to . . . hell."

"I'll find out anyway," Fargo said. "I'm going on to Meridian." Odds were, whoever didn't want him there would make themselves known.

"Tried to . . . help . . . pard," Clemens managed to get out as more blood oozed.

"I still need a name."

Clemens didn't answer.

Standing, Fargo aimed his Colt at the center of Clemens's forehead. "Reckon I'll put you out of your misery, then."

For the first time fear showed in the other's eyes.

"You said . . . you'd wait . . . and bury me."

"I said I'd bury you," Fargo agreed. "I never said I'd wait around for you to die."

"Bastard."

"Nice meeting you, too." Fargo stroked the trigger.